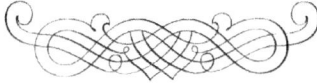

Published by Five Pyramids Press, Suite 1a 34 West Street,
Retford, England, DN22 6ES
ISBN: 9798298162777

RESENT

Emmy Ellis

Chapter One

Dear Diary,
My name is Karen Marie Livingstone, and one day I'm going to be really, really rich. I'm ten years old today, and I go to the primary school up the road. I haven't got any friends, but that's okay, because if I had friends then I'd have to

share my money when I'm rich, and I don't want to, I want to keep it all to myself. Actually, I'd share some with Dad but not Mum.

Dad's my friend, and he makes me laugh. The best days are when we go out on our own together and Mum stays at home. If she's around then she gets a lot of attention, like she's his whole sunshine and I'm not. She's pretty and always looks nice. She's like one of those models in the paper.

I don't think I'm going to grow up to be like that, she said I'm not pretty enough, but when I'm rich I can have my nails and hair done and buy lovely clothes and shoes, and the makeup will make me look nice.

I better go. Dad's calling me. We're going to the park.

Love from,
Karen Marie Livingstone

Karen skipped along the pavement, her pigtails swinging. She glanced over her shoulder to see how far behind Dad was, and he stuck his thumb on the end of his nose and wiggled his fingers because he'd caught her looking. She laughed, turned to face ahead and raced on, her legs hot in her jeans.

She'd wanted to put on the pretty dress Dad had got her from the lady at work whose little girl had grown out of it, but he'd said no because it might get dirty at the park, and anyway, it was for wearing later at her birthday dinner, which Mum was cooking while they were out. She didn't cook much usually, Dad did it when he got home from work, but today was special, and she wasn't half bad at making sausage and oven chips with beans, Karen's favourite dinner. She wouldn't ever say she'd prefer chips from the chippy, because Mum and Dad struggled for money—they talked about it enough for her to know it got "really bad" sometimes—but yeah, she'd love chippy chips.

She rounded the corner at the end of the street, then ran into the park entrance. There were so many people, probably because it was Saturday. Mothers sat with buggies on picnic blankets or on benches round the edge, watching their children, and it upset Karen a bit that hers wasn't there. Mind you, she was used to it, Mum not getting involved, and at least Dad had come. Mum was never much fun at the park anyway. She never pushed Karen's swing high enough, and she fussed about her hair if the wind blew or if it rained a bit. The lady next door said Mum shouldn't have had children if she wasn't prepared to dig in. Karen didn't think she was supposed to have heard that over the back garden fence.

"She's one of those high-maintenance tarts," the woman had said. "Looks pretty but useless anywhere outside the bedroom."

Karen played on the swings. Dad leaned against the basketball post, his arms folded, then his attention was drawn to the tune of the ice cream van. Karen glanced at him to check if she could have one, and he fished in his pockets, staring at the money on his palm and then looking up at her and nodding. Her tummy rolled over with excitement. She ran over to him, smiling, grabbing his hand, and they walked out of the park together, catching sight of the van that had parked just up the road. Dad bought her a 99 with a Flake in it, lots of strawberry sauce dripping, but he didn't have one himself.

He never had one, but he always stared at hers like he wanted it.

"Do you want a lick of mine?" she asked.

"Birthday girls don't have to share."

"But you never want me to share."

"That's because you deserve everything all to yourself."

They returned to the park and sat on a bench that was warm from the sun while she ate, and she didn't reckon she'd had a better day in her life. She'd got a diary, some socks, and a new T-shirt for her birthday, then there was the ice cream, and Dad had said there would be cake after dinner, he'd got one cheap down the bakery. It had been in the cabinet for a few days, but it would be all right because it was covered in pink butter icing so would still be soft inside.

After her ice cream, she played at the park for a bit longer, then Dad said it was time to go. She walked home holding his hand, hoping she never forgot how it felt around hers. Indoors, the smell of dinner filled the air, and they sat at the table while Mum dished up. Dad stuck a fat white candle in the cake, one of the ones they used when the electric went out, and they sang 'Happy Birthday'.

Karen blew the candle out and made a wish: Please make me rich!

Chapter Two

The moon cast its silvery glow, the pool of blood on the cobblestones glistening. There was so much history here, horses' hoofs once clip-clopping over the stones, a market held on this spot a hundred-odd years ago. Where one of the three warehouses stood, there used to be a tavern called Ye Olde Trough, travellers stopping by to allow their horses to drink. It had long ago burned down, its thatched roof catching fire from some twat smoking in the attic, eight people dead. Nathaniel always got spooked in that particular warehouse, as if their ghosts lingered, and a chill never failed to go up his spine.

But he had another ghost to worry about now.

The body of Paddy Winchester lay on the ground, and if Nathaniel didn't get rid of it quickly, make it disappear, someone might come along and see it. See him standing over it in his black clothes and balaclava. The news of the death would get the police poking their noses in, and he couldn't have that. He'd been running the Greaves Estate for his father for quite a while, getting rid of people quietly behind the scenes while pretending he was the type of man who didn't want any violence, so to have it be known that a death had occurred on Greaves property… Fuck that.

The police weren't wanted around here.

On cue, a siren pierced the night, disturbing the stillness and his equilibrium. He held his breath, pulse thudding. If coppers were coming, then he was well and truly fucked. This courtyard and the horseshoe of warehouses surrounding it belonged to his father, Henry, and if the pigs swarmed in, Nathaniel would be in trouble in more ways than one.

Henry would mete out punishment, and Nathaniel would be the recipient.

He hated his father with a passion and couldn't wait to kill the bastard.

He was anxious someone was hanging around, watching him, maybe even filming him. For all he knew a TikTok post could go up, and it would look like he was the guilty one. It wouldn't take much to frame him. He stared into the deep shadows closest to the buildings, searching for whoever had murdered Paddy. That was supposed to be Karen's job, his stepmother, the woman he was having an affair with.

They had two things in common: they were similar ages and they hated Henry Greaves. A few minutes ago, Karen had said via text that she hadn't killed Paddy, and Nathaniel hadn't, so who the hell was it? Nathaniel had promised he'd help Karen get this done—Paddy was the kind of bloke who liked touching arses when he hadn't been given permission. Some people didn't take kindly to that sort of thing, Karen in particular, and wanted proper retribution. All right, she'd got it because Paddy was dead anyway, but things might get sticky considering an unknown had committed the murder.

Unless it was the person whose arse he'd touched.

Or Karen was lying to him.

The siren went off again, but it was quieter, moving away from the scene, so Nathaniel relaxed a little. This area was quiet after midnight, so the killer would have been able to approach and get away without being spotted, just like Nathaniel and Karen had discussed when she was going to do it. Whoever had been here tonight had either known there weren't any cameras or they'd covered their faces. Going by Karen's messages, she'd come here to meet him and had found Paddy dead. Nathaniel had been inside one of the warehouses, as arranged, waiting for Paddy to turn up for their agreed meeting—and Karen, who'd been running late.

It had gone tits up to be fair.

He recalled their exchange.

NATHANIEL: WHERE THE FUCK ARE YOU?

KAREN: WHERE ARE YOU?

NATHANIEL: IN THE WAREHOUSE, LIKE WE SAID.

KAREN: SO YOU DIDN'T DO IT OUTSIDE?

NATHANIEL: WHAT?

KAREN: HE'S ON THE GROUND. HOW COULD YOU MISS HIM?

NATHANIEL: SHIT, I DIDN'T PUT HIM THERE.

KAREN: WELL, IT WASN'T ME! AND YOU'RE NOT MEANT TO BE TEXTING ME!

He sensed her tension in those words, how she'd be afraid it would all go wrong now another person, or persons, were in the mix. Nathaniel wasn't exactly throwing a party about it himself, and it wasn't like anyone was going to grass on the killer, not to him anyway, because they'd know he'd be gunning for them for doing it on his father's property.

He crouched to inspect the blood on Paddy's shirt. It looked like he'd been stabbed, hence the pool of red beneath him, which appeared black in the night. At least there wasn't a bullet casing to find or an obvious bullet hole in one of the cobblestones if it had gone straight through the body. He was going to have to get a move on; despite this area being deserted, the way his luck had gone tonight, someone would come along and see him.

Understandably, considering what Karen had been through, she had a thing about perverts not being allowed to get away with it. He had a feeling that any time she heard about an injustice, especially when it had to do with men forcing themselves on women, she'd be running to him and asking—or more like telling—him to get rid of them. That wasn't a problem, he had the perfect place to dispose of bodies, but once his father was dead, he'd prefer it if he wasn't running around chasing sexual deviants.

This particular sexual deviant was Nathaniel's top priority, so he'd better get a move on. He dragged Paddy into warehouse two, the scent of Nathaniel's aftershave lingering from when he'd been in there earlier, waiting for Karen. It reminded him not to put it on when he was going out on a job like this—leaving a signature scent in different circumstances might be his downfall.

His father would say he still had so much to learn.

Nathaniel would want to tell him to fuck off.

In the dark, he put Paddy on a tarpaulin covered in a plastic sheet which he'd already laid out in preparation, rolling him up in it, folding the ends over and over then taping them.

Paddy was ready for his next destination. Nathaniel had a man who worked for him. Shane Best owned a factory, and put it this way, one of his smelters wasn't used for metal.

He opened the adjoining door into warehouse number one on the left where he'd parked a stolen vehicle in readiness. He put Paddy in the large boot, shut the lid, and returned to number two. At the back stood a row of three metal sinks, each of them with big black buckets on the draining boards, squirts of bleach in the bottoms. He ran the hot taps until the water became scalding and then put the buckets beneath the streams. Once they were full, he carried two out into the courtyard, going inside to collect a stiff-bristled broom. He got to work, scrubbing the cobblestones, diluting the blood. He left the two empty buckets refilling while he took the third back out, pouring the bleach water over the area. He did the same with the other two, shunting the water towards one of the drain grates. He couldn't hang around to wait for it to dry, he had to get rid of Paddy, but he'd come back later and check that none of the blood was still visible.

He took the buckets and broom inside and locked warehouse two, then put them in the stolen car. They'd be destroyed with Paddy. He was just about to click the fob on his key ring to raise the roller door when a streak of light flashed through the windows, illuminating warehouse one. He darted behind the vehicle, looking through the window. The lights moved, the rumble of an engine revving, and then the darkness was back.

Whoever it was had gone. Maybe they'd gone the wrong way and used the courtyard as a turning point. Whatever had happened, Nathaniel was going to have to check before he took the chance of leaving. Taking a risk with a dead body in the boot wasn't his idea of a good decision.

Heart pattering an unsteady rhythm, he left the building, keeping to the shadows on his way to the open metal gates that secured the warehouses from the cobblestone road. He peered out, wincing at the nearby church clock chiming the hour—two in the morning now. He looked left, spotting taillights, pinpricks that were nothing for him to worry about. That car was long gone.

He returned to the warehouse and got in the motor, opening the roller door and backing out.

On the road, he clicked the fob to close the roller, then got out and shut the gates. They were usually left open, but he didn't want to risk someone seeing the wet ground while he was gone, and he reminded himself going forward that the gates really ought to be locked after business had been concluded each day. Leaving them open had been his father's idea, he'd hated having to get out of his car to open or close them, but considering what warehouse three contained, why invite burglars? Guns were big business, and hidden inside a safe or not, with the gates open they were easier pickings.

Using backstreets where he knew there was no CCTV, he drove to the outskirts of the Estate. He parked up at the factory and used his key to unlock the creaky gates, then drove through and got out yet again to lock them behind him. He found a spot down the side of the building and cut the engine there, sending a message to Best to let him know he was going to be using the smelter.

He got out and opened the wooden door, propping it back with the little hook on the wall, then switched off the alarm, silencing the beeping noise coming from the control panel. He collected the packet of Paddy from the boot and took him inside, placing him on the floor and locking them in. He dragged him through to the area where the assembly line had been abandoned by the employees earlier, their hard work forgotten until the morning when they started up all over again. He tugged the body further, into the room that held the smelter he was allowed to use.

The ones still in use were kept running as it was a long and costly process to keep shutting them down and restarting. Two of them had been permanently shut off, though, due to the cost of electricity.

He switched on the light, the old fluorescent tube flickering, creating creepy shadows on the walls. He ignored it and put Paddy in the smelter. He'd forced someone in there alive once, such a bastard move, but it had served the intended purpose—to ensure Best understood that Nathaniel was the boss around here and if he didn't behave, then he'd get burned to death in his own factory.

Nathaniel took his phone out and checked the time, also looking for messages from Karen. There were none. He didn't have to think too hard as to why she could have been late arriving at the warehouses. She'd been putting drugs in his father's whisky prior to bed, but sometimes the old boy got randy before sleep pulled at him, and he expected her to perform her wifely duties, which these days amounted to a blow job.

Nathaniel was supposed to be taking Karen to Italy soon. The story for the masses was that she'd be running a business over there for Henry, but in reality, he wanted Nathaniel to kill her.

Fuck that.

Nathaniel had asked the twins from the Cardigan Estate to help, but they still hadn't got back to him with their answer. He could understand why they'd be reticent to get involved with another leader's business, but he hoped they'd do the right thing. If he hadn't heard by tomorrow then he'd get hold of them. He wanted to move on this quickly, get rid of Henry before he decided to kill Karen sooner. Henry wasn't exactly known for his patience, and if she pissed him off enough, he was likely to whip a gun out and shoot her in the head where she stood, fuck the consequences.

Nathaniel had grown to care about her more than he'd expected, and the idea of her dying when he'd just allowed himself to fall in love with her wasn't something he even wanted to contemplate.

The sudden clap of footsteps against concrete had him opening one of the doors that led to another room. He hid, standing so he could look through the gap at the hinges.

"Nath?"

Relief powered into him. "I'm here." He stepped out from behind the door. "What have I told you about creeping up on me here? Fucking send a message to say you're on your way next time. And what are you doing here anyway?"

"I've got someone of my own to pop in there."

It wasn't a surprise. Nathaniel employed Best to get rid of the rats on the good ship Greaves, and two of the filthy vermin were due to be cremated soon. Dare he hope Best had got lucky and finally killed the Carter brothers? Karen had been on his back about that just yesterday.

"Who is it?" Nathaniel asked.

"Carter, but only one of them. Rob. His brother ran off before I could shoot him. I caught them beating up that old dear who lives down Rectory Place, opposite the Bell. I was just leaving the pub at the same time as the Carters, gearing myself up to kill the bastards, and she came out of her house to shout at them to stop singing. They were being pretty loud to be honest. They went over to her and started throwing punches. I grabbed Oscar and threw him off. He saw it was me and legged it. I gripped Rob up and dragged him away. Did my usual by setting off a couple of fireworks then shot him in the fucking head down an alley. Put him in my van then went back to Rectory to see if she was all right. She moaned about the fireworks scaring her, didn't seem bothered about the big bruise on her face, but I rang her a taxi, sent her off to the hospital. Who have you got in there?" He gestured to the smelter.

"Never you mind."

"Probably better I don't know. Right, I'll go and get Rob."

Nathaniel needed to get the buckets and the broom, so he followed Best out. He helped him carry Rob, who was a big heavy bastard, then went back for the stuff. While everything burned, Best drank from his hip flask and went through his plan for Oscar.

"I can't do it tonight because it'll be too obvious if both of them disappear at the same time."

19

"Yep, two brothers out on the piss; both of them going missing is a bit of a stretch." Nathaniel was going to have to placate Karen, get her down off her high horse when she heard only one brother was dead. "Did you tell the old lady to keep her mouth shut on who attacked her?"

"Yeah, I said you'd be round with a little present."

Nathaniel nodded. "I'll do that. What's her name?"

"Beatrice Brown."

"Okay. Listen, I need to go, so speak soon."

He drove back to the warehouse. The cobblestones had dried in the hot night, and he shone his torch over the patch where Paddy had lain. Thankfully, the stones weren't discoloured from the blood.

He locked the gates and sent Karen a message to meet him. He didn't want to go to his father's house where she currently waited for him, even though he needed a shower and a change of clothes which he kept in the room he used to have before he'd moved out. It was better that they chatted in a place where Henry wouldn't wake up and overhear them.

Not that he wakes up with the pills she gives him.

Still, better to be safe than sorry, especially with the potential of Karen flipping her lid that Oscar Carter was still alive and kicking.

He stuck his phone back in his pocket and drove away, heading for the pub he owned not far from Henry's place. Karen could walk there in about three minutes. He was going to do up the Galway Arms. The place had been abandoned for years after it had flooded and the owner had failed to get an insurance payout—he'd forgotten to pay his premiums. Nathaniel had bought it for a song.

He parked in the street round the back that had no houses. He inhaled a deep breath before he got out, then unlocked the gate and walked through the yard, turned his key in the door, and stepped inside to find Karen standing there in the corridor, waiting.

"What the fuck is going *on*?" she whispered.

Chapter Three

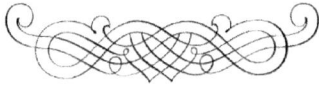

In the dim bar, they sat at a table that had one leg shorter than the others so it wobbled. Karen had found an old cardboard beer mat amongst the debris on the floor and folded it into quarters to level things out.

This pub was an utter shit state, but it had served a purpose for months, the place where they discussed all the things they couldn't say at home. She wouldn't put it past Henry to have listening devices there as well as the cameras she already knew about. Unfortunately, this was also one of the places where they met up for sex. It wasn't somewhere Karen would have chosen, but in order to keep Nathaniel on side she felt being intimate with him as often as possible was the best way to go.

She wasn't who he thought she was, and every day she had to remind herself that was okay. It was perfectly fine to use someone's feelings and emotions if it meant she got what she wanted. The problem was, he'd been showing her lately how much he cared about her, and little pinches of guilt created knots in her stomach when she thought about how mean she was being.

But needs must.

She sniffed in distaste. A suffocating cocktail of dirt, dust, and stagnant water hung in the air. God knew what insects lived here, not to mention mice and rats, something she tried not to think about when her knickers were around her ankles. Random debris littered the floor—newspapers, broken wooden chair-back spindles, a smashed glass or two, indeterminate other stuff she couldn't even try to put a name to. But the cobwebs were the worst. She hated the thought of the spiders coming back to their homes and sitting there, watching her, and if they weren't in the webs, there was more potential for them to crawl on her.

Or in my knickers.

She shuddered.

The thick curtains had been drawn. A single bulb flashed intermittently overhead, pissing her off. If there was one thing that was guaranteed to give her a migraine, it was stupid flashing lights. She sighed and put her phone torch on then got up to switch off the main light. Okay, it was now creepier than before with only a small amount of light between her and Nathaniel, eerie shadows at their backs, but she couldn't concentrate with that flickering going on.

This meeting was in contrast to the previous ones. They weren't discussing an imminent murder or how they were going to get rid of Henry. They weren't going to have sex. Instead, it was to discuss how the *fuck* someone else had killed Paddy—how they'd even known where he'd be. Maybe someone else had planned to murder him all along and had just happened to be following him to the warehouses. And he could have opened his mouth, of course; his killer might have overheard him talking to someone else about meeting up with Nathaniel at the warehouses.

That could pose a bloody big problem, and her mouth dried from the speck of fear that had the potential to grow into a bloody great ball if she didn't rein in her emotions. She'd brought a bag with her containing coffees in thermal cups, something she could thank her past self for now that her tongue had lost all its moisture. She'd had a full carafe of coffee on the go while she'd been waiting for Nathaniel at the house so had quickly made up the drinks and then run all the way here. She thought she'd be late again but had arrived first.

"Tell me what happened on your end," he said.

"I was late because of *him*. He wanted a blow job before his whisky." She got perverse pleasure from telling Nathaniel things like that, knowing how much they upset him.

She didn't think she was going to make it to Heaven.

Nathaniel winced; was the image of her down on her knees, serving his wrinkly father, flickering through his mind? "I thought that's what must have happened."

"Then he wanted to talk afterwards, saying he might ask the Carter brothers over again, another one of his stupid games where he threatens me, so it was getting close to midnight by the time he'd finally had his drink and conked out. I had to run all the way to the warehouses, and when I got there I found Paddy in the courtyard. I'll admit I was naffed off; I thought you'd murdered him because you were annoyed I was late, but then you said you hadn't done it so…"

Her words had come out in a rush, and she took a moment to inhale some steady breaths. This was all so exciting, but at the same time it could mess everything up. All those plans she'd made…

"How did they do it?" She had an idea, going by what she'd seen of the body, but she wanted to be sure.

"He was stabbed."

"I thought so. Did you clean up or is that something we still need to do?"

"I've sorted it, and he's in the smelter. Best turned up while I was there. He gave me some good news in this shitshow of a mess."

"What's that then?"

"We finally got Rob Carter."

Relieved, Karen let her shoulders drop down. She'd wanted those men dead for such a long time. Bastards, the pair of them. "What about Oscar?"

"He got away, but his time will come. Plus, like Best reminded me, it's better that they weren't killed at the same time."

"It makes no difference when they were killed if neither of their bodies will ever be found."

"Okay then, I'll rephrase it: it's better that they don't go missing at the same time."

She rolled her eyes, annoyed. They'd been over this before. "Them going missing together just gives it more credibility; people will think they fucked off together to start again elsewhere, but never mind, I'll just have to wait for Oscar to die…"

The brothers had raped her—Henry's orders. When he'd told her to put on sexy underwear, she'd thought she was having an evening with her husband, which was something she'd never enjoyed, but it was a means to an end. She'd become a master at faking it. In the bedroom it became clear what was really going on. The Carter brothers had stood either side of the bed, naked. Henry had shut the door, locked it, and sat in the corner to watch.

He'd paid them afterwards.

It had been a brutal attack, no other words for it, something Henry had threatened her with a repeat of afterwards. "If you don't do what I want then Rob and Oscar will be back… If you don't get down on your knees then Rob and Oscar will be back…"

He had no idea that she was being paid to endure all this crap from him, that she'd been paid to marry the old bastard, and when he was dead, she had fifty grand coming her way. He thought he held all the cards, but she did.

"Does Best know who you put in the smelter?" she asked.

"I didn't think he needed to know our business."

"Tell me about what happened to Rob."

Nathaniel explained everything, and she enjoyed listening to it, imagining Rob's head had being blown off, or part of it anyway, bits of his brain going everywhere. She smiled at the image of his body being burned, his skin blistering like pork crackling. Best always cleaned up after himself; he carried huge flagons of water in the back of his van with some clever contraption attached so he could use a hose pipe. Couple that with the fireworks going off to disguise gunshots, and no one would even know Rob had been killed down the alley.

"I was just thinking about the next time Oscar's in the Bell and Rob isn't there," she said. "Because Best was the one to pull them off the old lady, won't Oscar have something to say to him? It'll draw attention."

"Best will act casual and say he marched Rob off and sent him on his way, that he doesn't know where he went after that. Don't worry about it."

But she did worry. She hated the thought of the truth getting out about what the Carters had done to her, although knowing Henry, he probably bragged about it. There could be numerous people who were in the know, walking past her in town, and she'd have no idea they were laughing at her behind her back for staying with such a sadistic man. Best was aware because Nathaniel had explained everything prior to giving him the job of murdering the Carters. He trusted Best, otherwise he wouldn't have considered giving him gigs like that, but Karen wasn't so sure if *she* could trust him. She felt Best would turn to whoever offered him the most money and protection. At the moment it was Nathaniel, but what if Henry got wind of Best helping his son out and he poked his nose in, giving him a better deal?

She trusted no one but herself.

Henry and Nathaniel had spent their lives evading the law, evading those residents who could get them into trouble, and now that Karen was so close to getting what she wanted, she was afraid it would all go wrong at the last minute. She and Nathaniel could kill Henry themselves, or pay Best to do it, but Nathaniel's idea of involving the twins was a much better option. Them doing it would draw suspicion away from Nathaniel and Karen.

It pissed her off that they hadn't got in contact with Nathaniel yet, but they weren't the type of people she could march up to and demand answers. George would likely flick her away, as if she were an annoying fly.

"We need to find out who killed Paddy and whether they know we intended to get there first," Nathaniel said. "I'm worried that he told someone I asked to meet him at the warehouses, even though I told him to keep it to himself."

That was always going to be the tricky part of the equation. You could tell someone all you liked not to open their mouth, but it was their choice whether they obeyed you or not.

Nathaniel had said he had a job for him, lots of cash in hand, and Paddy being Paddy, the greedy bastard had agreed straight away. Someone else had wanted him dead and had used the opportunity to do it in the yard so it would look like it was Nathaniel. They weren't to know it was going to be Karen's first kill.

"Did Best know our plans?" she asked.

"No—I've already told you I thought it was better that he didn't know who I'd put in the smelter."

"Sorry, I forgot." She hadn't, she was just testing him.

They talked for a long time, until fingers of the dawn daylight poked around the dusty curtains. Karen switched the torch app off, her phone battery low. She got up and opened one of the curtains a tad, staring through the grimy window at the houses opposite.

"What's the weather like out there?" Nathaniel asked.

"I think it's going to be another hot day."

"We'd better get going."

It was a given that Henry never woke up until after nine o'clock every day, and while it was only five now, she got jittery at the thought of him finding her gone. Even worse, watching her out of the window as she went up the street as though on the walk of shame. She often wondered whether he knew she was seeing Nathaniel, which was why he wanted to send her to her death in Italy, although he'd apparently done the same to Nathaniel's mother when he'd got bored of her. Killed her, although she hadn't had the luxury of it being abroad. With regards to Karen, he'd probably get smug satisfaction out of the fact that his own son was killing his wife.

Such a bastard.

"I'll pop round later, at lunchtime," Nathaniel said.

She nodded, although they'd both be playing different roles then, her the stepmother, him the stepson. Knowing him, he'd leave here, have a quick shower and a two-hour nap at his posh flat, then set off in search of whoever could tell him something about Paddy Winchester's murderer.

Many people talked for a price.

She went over and kissed him on the top of the head. She put the coffee cups back in the bag and walked out the back of the pub and past the stolen car that he'd get rid of today. She hugged herself on the walk home, not wanting to go inside the house that had seen so many horrors, mainly inflicted on her. But she was nearing the end of the nightmare now.

She went in through the patio doors at the rear, closing them and then standing quietly to listen. Not a sound. She plugged her phone in and placed it on the worktop in the kitchen, switching the sounds and vibration off. Upstairs, she looked in on Henry who lay on his back, snoring with his mouth open. She'd never loved him, he'd just been her ticket to riches.

Nearly there.

She went into the dressing room next door and picked out some clothes. She used the main bathroom instead of the en suite, even though it was doubtful Henry would hear her. The capsule tablets she opened and emptied into his drinks were strong. She showered and got dressed, going back to the kitchen to make some instant porridge and coffee for breakfast. She put some frozen croissants in the oven for Henry.

She sat at the island, so tired. Maybe she'd sleep on the sofa until he woke.

She stared around at the kitchen she'd been so eager to cook in when she'd first seen it. The marble worktops must have cost a fortune, as must the marble flooring, the pendant lights above the island worth more than her old monthly wage. She'd looked them up on Google. During the spare time she had when Henry and Nathaniel were busy, she came here to cook and bake, wanting to create the same atmosphere she'd had as a child when Dad had cooked, the smells of pastries and dinners giving her comfort.

Such a shame that the home she'd tried to create here had gone so wrong—it was all just an illusion, she'd known it would be from the start, and how naive she'd been to think this would be easy. She'd had no idea who Henry was, the *real* man behind the façade he presented to the rest of the world. She'd been put in her place pretty quickly—she was at the bottom of the pecking order, no doubt about it. She was nothing but a housekeeper and someone to suck his cock, but then didn't she deserve to be treated that way, considering she'd walked in here with a view to relieving Henry of everything he owned?

Served herself right, really.

She glanced towards the window. The sun had risen even more since her mad dash from the pub, shining on the grass and the leaves of the tropical-like trees—Henry's oasis that he'd tended to himself before he'd grown increasingly old in his behaviours. Now he sat and watched someone else do it, a gardener called Ken Fox— Foxy—who Nathaniel had employed. Foxy was actually an old school friend of his, someone he trusted to keep Henry occupied during the times he had to speak to Karen alone.

The tinny sound of the letterbox flap had her stomach flipping over. It was too early for the postman. She rushed to the front of the house, and at the living room window caught sight of a hooded figure at the bottom of the driveway, their back to her, turning left, then obscured by the high hedge border. She ran upstairs as quietly as she could and stared out of the front bedroom window. She'd made it just in time to see over the hedge. A man got in the passenger side of a red Fiesta which set off slowly, the engine quiet.

She returned downstairs to the hallway and stared at a folded piece of paper on the mat. Its presence jarred her—she knew straight away it would have words on it she didn't want to read. Karen collected Marigold gloves from the kitchen and went back into the hallway, glancing upstairs just in case Henry had appeared at the top. She turned back to the mat, her heart racing as she reached for the piece of paper, opening it out to read it.

We want paying for the Paddy job. 20 grand. Leave it behind the empty beer kegs in the yard at the Galway Arms, tonight at 10. Don't hang around. Drop it and go, otherwise Karen's next.

The paper shook in her hand, the crackling sound of it too loud. Her mind raced. Who the fuck had sent it? And why was she next? Did the person know she was supposed to be the one to kill Paddy? Had Nathaniel told someone of their plans? No, he'd said he hadn't told a soul. She racked her brain to remember where they'd discussed everything—definitely at the Galway, but here, too, when they'd been whispering in the kitchen with the radio on and Henry had sat in the orangery watching Foxy mow the grass. Was it like she'd thought and there were listening devices here?

Whoever it was, they were aware that Karen and Nathaniel met at the Galway, when all along they'd thought they were being clever in using the empty pub. What if it was someone who lived in the houses opposite? Could they have got curious as to why Nathaniel and Karen kept turning up there, and they'd crept in, standing in the corridor and listening? Nathaniel hadn't always locked the door when they had gone inside.

Shit.

With that in mind, she forced down a whimper that had been threatening to pop out ever since the letterbox had flapped. It was as if a dark cloud hovered now, the note bringing it into the house to follow her around for the rest of the day. She was going to be a nervous wreck until the money had been handed over.

Panic spread through her body, and she swore the walls were closing in. What if whoever was driving the Fiesta had only gone round the back and they were intending to break in any second? Her imagination ran riot at the thought of two people shielded by the high hedges of the garden, waiting for their moment to come in. It wasn't going to do her any good tormenting herself, so she rushed back into the kitchen and took a picture of the note, sending it to Nathaniel over WhatsApp.

She waited for some time for a response, but like she'd thought earlier, he was probably napping by now. She phoned him, but he didn't answer. She unplugged the phone charger, walked into the living room, and plugged it in by the armchair she sat in. She rested her head back and closed her eyes, trying to dismiss her fears, trying to get at least a little bit of sleep despite her worries, but the sound of a floorboard creaking above had her shooting to her feet.

Either Henry was awake earlier than usual or someone else was upstairs. She quickly deleted the photo she'd sent to Nathaniel and the evidence of her connecting a call and sending a message to him. Henry had asked to look through her phone at random intervals before. She remembered she'd left the note on the side in the kitchen and rushed in there to get it. She put it in her bra and walked to the bottom of the stairs, looking up.

No one was there.

Shaking, she returned to the living room and accessed the security app, watching the recorded footage. She checked it. No one had been recorded breaking in, so it must be Henry who was awake. How, when she'd drugged him so much?

She went upstairs, finding him asleep in the same position he'd been in before. Had she imagined the creak of the floorboard? Was it the hot water in the pipes? She checked the rest of the house, ending up back downstairs. Maybe Henry had turned over in bed, then ended upon his back again anyway.

She sat in the armchair, staring into the middle distance, frightened of an unknown person who had plans to kill her if the money wasn't delivered. Nathaniel would make sure it was taken to the pub yard, she had no doubt of that, but there was no way the person would be walking away with it.

They were going to have to meet at the Galway Arms today and make new plans. She'd tell Henry she was going shopping. Foxy was coming to do the gardening this afternoon, so her husband would be occupied.

She closed her eyes again, hyperaware of the goosebumps on her skin and the chill racing up it. She stiffened her spine. There was no way she'd be a victim, not after she'd clawed her way up from a poor childhood into an adult life of riches.

Whoever was toying with them had better watch their back.

The smoke alarm went off, and she launched herself out of the chair.

Shit, she'd forgotten about the croissants!

Chapter Four

*D*ear Diary,
   I fucking HATE my life and being a teenager. I resent everything about it. I don't think anyone gets just how much. I can't stand waking up every day, facing the same shit. I don't sleep very well, staring at the ceiling in the dark. I'm

only tired when it's time to get up, and then I just want to hide under the covers and never come out. Or not come out until I'm an adult when everything will be better.

It feels like I'm walking round in fog all the time. That's got to be the lack of sleep, or maybe it's the hormones the science teacher banged on about the other day. That's her answer for everything, hormones. Peter Shore was allowed to get away with something because of hormones. Cally Grey swore at a teacher, and she got away with that, too. But if I did it? Yeah, you can guess what would happen. I'd be suspended. Mum would be brought in for a meeting about my behaviour. God, school is seriously shit with all the rules, but it seems like most of the others are coping all right, unless they're really good at hiding it. They're getting their work done, high scores, whereas I'm failing, falling well short of the mark.

But I've got an A level in sarcasm.

"Sarcasm isn't going to get you a job, though, is it, Karen?" That's what the headmaster said to me the other day after he'd told me off for said sarcasm.

He just doesn't get it. No one understands me, apart from Dad, and he's ill, so I can't tell him my problems.

He's going to die, I know it. I'll be left here with a mother who doesn't give a fuck about me, only about herself. Her selfishness has become more apparent as I've got older. I suppose I can understand more now. Why does Dad stay with her? What is it about her that makes him want to keep her around? I can't stand her personally, and I'll never understand what he sees in her.

But back to the subject of him dying. Mum said he isn't that far gone yet, but he's probably told her to lie to me. Doesn't want me to worry, but I can see it in his eyes. They've gone dull, like who he is isn't even in his body anymore, if that makes sense.

I went into his bedroom the other day. It's weird because I can't remember it ever being a dining room now. Mum had the wallpaper ripped off by one of the neighbours down the road, the decorator bloke who did it for free, and now it's all white paint, which makes it look sterile, something that's really important apparently. He's got one of those drip things, a nurse comes every weekday to change the pouches that hang off it. Mum's been taught how to do it, too, for the weekends.

I have to admit, she's been pretty good at playing nursemaid, something I'd never have imagined her doing. Maybe it makes her look good. She gets a lot of attention off people for supposedly putting Dad first. She still has nice nail polish on, though, and her hair's always in place. No matter how much she tells people she's run off her feet looking after him, there's still time to pamper herself.

Why can't other people see that she's a liar?

There was talk of him going into a hospice — a conversation I probably wasn't supposed to have overheard — and I'm not stupid, I know what that means, but he must want to die at home. I feel bad, but it'll be creepy here if he does.

That wasn't a nice thing to say, but these things pop into my head. I can't seem to stop them. And I keep waiting to feel something other than anger that he got ill. When he dies I'll be with the wrong parent. It should be Mum who's dying, not him. He cares about me more than she does.

We might not have much money, but you wouldn't be able to tell if you looked at my mother. But I thought, because she's the type not to want to get her hands dirty, that she'd never have sat by Dad's bed the majority of the time, reading to him, watching telly with him, talking about the times before I was born when they'd had a laugh. It had come across that she wished I hadn't been born, I'd spoiled it all, but I couldn't say anything because I was listening outside the door. I'd spied on a private moment, which was fucking shit of me really.

I'd better go, I've got homework to do. Crap algebra.

Love from,
Karen Marie Livingstone

Karen hadn't expected anyone at school to give a flying fuck that her father was dying, but somehow news had spread, and people stared at her funny—more than they had before. It was like her world had turned to shadows and there was a spotlight on her, making her more visible. A couple of girls thought it was amusing to whisper taunts, saying she was Daddy's girl and what would she do without him. These poisoned arrows were launched deliberately to hurt her, for whatever reason, and she couldn't understand for the life of her why. She hadn't done anything at this school other than mind her own business, but then maybe people thought she was being snooty because she hadn't made friends.

She'd learned from primary school that wasn't something she was prepared to do now. Friends turned on you, they weren't to be trusted. It was better that she stayed by herself.

Then jokes came, boys mimicking choking to death by coughing, so it was obvious they'd found out her dad had lung cancer. Every time they did it she imagined Dad doing the same in his bed, trying to catch his breath, panicking because he couldn't get enough air in. Karen was a bitch and thought some horrible things at times, especially about her mother, but she couldn't imagine saying the things that had been said to her or pretending to choke. What kind of people were they? Worse than her, and that was saying something. At least she kept all of her spiteful comments to herself.

Someone had put a picture on her desk of a cemetery. Whoever had drawn it had shitty art skills. What pleasure did they get out of picking on her like this? She was an easy target, but did that mean she should put up with what they were doing? Fucking bastards, the lot of them. She could go and tell a teacher, but what was the point? The kids would probably bully her for that, too. And in her experience, the teachers had never wanted to know when she told them about bullies before. She was so tired of fighting her own battles.

Maybe this was her fault for behaving as if everyone was beneath her, when in reality, she was likely one of the poorest. If she didn't nick her clothes from the shops in town, she'd never have anything that was in fashion. Her shoes let her down so much, the ones for school scuffed where she'd had them so long.

She'd asked Mum if she could have one of her pairs, but she'd said no.

Why was everyone so cruel?

Chapter Five

George and Greg had been in the big house on the Greaves Estate before, and they'd also been in the orangery, basically a conservatory with a sofa and two reclining chairs, a coffee table, and a few hanging plants. George remembered the wife, Karen, watering those plants last time, clearly trying to listen in on their conversation. Henry had shooed her out, and he'd mentioned sending her to Italy soon where she'd end up dead.

Although he didn't know they were aware of that.

When they'd left the house, his son, Nathaniel, had come outside to say he couldn't be the one to kill Karen and he needed them to kill Henry instead. George and Greg were here to see if Henry spilled any information that would mean they'd have a good excuse to kill him—and an explanation for the other leaders. They could kill anyone on their own Estate if the fancy took them, but when it came to offing leaders, there really did need to be a good reason.

On the doorstep—the footage of their visit would be deleted later by Nathaniel—George studied the old boy to get a gauge on his mood today, as he hadn't given anything away so far other than to ask: "To what do I owe the pleasure?"

"We've been thinking about what you told us last time," George said.

"Last time?" Henry feigned being thick and not knowing what George was talking about.

George would indulge him for now. "About Karen and Italy."

Henry's eyes narrowed. "What about it?"

"Does she need to go to Italy? Can't it be done here? We'd be willing to lend a hand if it can."

Henry glanced at the camera above the door. "You'd better come in."

He showed them through the house and into the orangery again. Through the glass walls, the tropical garden was lush and very well looked after. Some of the big leaves looked like they'd been polished. This room was drenched in sunshine coming through the panes, light pooling on the furniture. Shadows from the leaves of a palm tree outside lay across the floor like a two-fingered salute. The silhouette of a bee hovered in front of the sofa, and George switched his attention to where it would be outside. It seemed to debate whether to land on a tall flower or not. The glossy leaves of some tree or other caught the light, and if he narrowed his gaze, he could pretend he was on some island getaway. He hadn't noticed this much detail before, wanting their business concluded so they could leave. This time he was here on a fact-finding mission so was more inclined to soak things in.

He had another quick look around for hidden cameras.

They all took a seat, Henry opening a fridge beside his chair. Had it been there previously? Who the fuck knew. He took out cans of Diet Coke, passing them out one at a time, George grateful for the cold drink as they'd been driving around for the past two hours and he'd forgotten to put some in the glove box.

George watched the old man struggling to open his can, what with those nasty gnarled fingers, and got pleasure in not offering to help him. Then again, it seemed he'd allowed Nathaniel to influence him on how to feel towards Henry. For all he knew, despite Henry being a known bastard, it could be Nathaniel who deserved to die.

In order to get a measure of the house's layout, it had been necessary to come here, plus he'd wanted to get more of a measure of Henry and not just take Nathaniel's word that he was an utter arsehole.

A panel of light slanted across the leader's face, chest, and the top part of the recliner, showcasing his wrinkles and faded, rheumy eyes. He didn't look like he'd harm a fly, and a lot of people didn't think he would—until they'd done something wrong that meant they had to have a face-to-face meeting with him, then it was a different story. People thought he was a kind old man, but fuck was he. In his white shirt, the sleeves rolled up to his elbows, and his dress trousers, he resembled anyone's granddad with his liver-spotted skin and grey hair, not some vicious killer.

"Where's Karen now?" Greg asked.

"Out doing some shopping, as usual. Nothing better to do than retail therapy, that one. It doesn't matter, the amount she spends barely makes a dent, but that's not the point, she's come to expect it. I don't think keeping the house clean and making my meals constitutes designer dresses and shoes and bags and whatever fuck else she buys, do you?"

"We don't tend to make a comment on marital relations," George said, "considering neither of us know what it's like to be married. We're not compatible with women."

"Are you a pair of queers then?"

"No, we're not compatible with men either. Relationships aren't for us."

"But you can have an opinion on mine, surely."

"I'd say if a woman did everything for me, giving up her right to have a job outside the home, then she's more than welcome to spend my money. That's not to say we don't understand how having a woman around can be...constraining. And limiting."

"Exactly that, and when they get boring, when all they've ended up being good at is giving a blow job, then they've got to go."

"Why not just divorce her?"

"Because she's the type to want to take half of everything. Quite frankly, I don't want to let it go. Why should I when I'm the one who worked for it? Plus, I reckon she's getting a bit too nosy about the guns we buy and sell. She wouldn't keep her gob shut if we split up."

"Not even if you threaten her?"

"I'm not sure. I'm ashamed to say I haven't quite got the gist of her. She sometimes looks like she's holding back, hiding something. So if you say it can be done in London, what do you propose? A little accident down by the Thames where she washes up on the shore for some poor bastard to find in the morning? Or will she get run over on a road with no cameras, the driver leaving her there as she struggles to breathe? Or maybe some cunt will follow her in the dark one night and rape the bitch up the arse."

Henry cackled, his eyes shut, some of his fillings visible on the bottom row where his mouth hung open. The way he'd described those death methods was as if he'd sat there and thought about them enough times that they were ingrained in his head. George understood that, he thought about methods of murder quite a lot, more than was healthy, but when he witnessed somebody else getting enjoyment from it, it seemed a lot more disturbing than when *he* did it.

Was that a case of do as I say, don't do as I do? Or was George having one of those epiphany moments where he saw himself through someone else's eyes?

I haven't got time to even give a shit what it is.

That was his excuse anyway.

Henry calmed down, taking a sip of Coke, his eyes streaming. He cuffed the tears away with the back of one hand, saying, "Oh dear," and then laughed again. George waited patiently for him to pack it in, or he pretended to be patient anyway, because in reality this man was getting right on his left bollock. He glanced at Greg to find that he was also annoyed.

Finally sobered enough to speak more than two words, Henry said, "Sorry, I got a bit carried away there. It reminded me of the night when I discussed my first wife being killed, that's Nathaniel's mother. She lasted a lot longer than Karen, I suppose because I needed her to bring the kid up and didn't want to let her go until all the dirty phases were over and done with, but she ended up in a car accident, wrapped around a tree."

He'd said it so calmly and without emotion that George believed Henry honestly didn't care that he'd taken a mother away from her child.

"Then a car accident is out for Karen," Greg said. "Two wives dying wrapped around a tree? Not good. Suspicious. In this day and age you could get away with her being raped and murdered on her way home from somewhere. These attacks happen so often, the police don't even bother to tell the public because it'd cause mass panic."

Henry's eyes widened. "I don't want Karen being in the news. This is why it was going to be done in Italy. For all anyone would know over here, she was running the business and didn't want to come back to London. I'd be going out there periodically to check on the new vineyard, so people would think I'd gone to visit her. Now I've had a chance to hear other options, I think we're better off sticking to my original idea, but thanks for the offer. I appreciate knowing you've got my back."

He gave a sly smile, and George wondered what the fuck the old boy was going to pull out of his sleeve next.

"I know you said you weren't compatible with women," Henry said, "but I don't suppose you'd fancy giving Karen a go before I pack her off, would you?"

"No thanks." George stood. "We'd best be off."

"I didn't offend you, did I?" Henry put his can down and pushed himself to standing with his palm's against the armrests of his chair. "She doesn't mind me sharing her, although she insists I sit and watch."

That wasn't the version Nathaniel had told them, but George wasn't about to correct him.

Greg rose to his feet. "We've got no time for that at the moment. Like my brother said, thanks, but we need to leave now."

"Fair enough, so long as we're still mates."

"Yep." George looked at Greg and gave a subtle nod: *We're killing this bastard ASAP*.

They followed Henry through the house, George resisting the urge to wallop the wanker on the back of the head so he flew forward and smacked his face on the front door handle, breaking his nose. He blinked away the visual to find Henry standing with the door open, grinning and nodding as he gestured them outside. George couldn't wait to breathe some fresh air. The oxygen in the house was tainted by the breath Henry exhaled. Poison, George would swear it.

Chapter Six

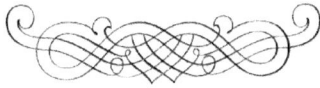

B est walked up the street towards the dilapidated Galway Arms, where the residents opposite likely had memories full of ghosts from the past, customers who'd spilled out of the doorway, drunk as lords, disrupting their quiet evenings at home. The street reminded him of an old mining town where his nan and granddad used to live, the houses a snaking line of terraces, the road itself made of cobblestones. The Greaves Estate had a lot of those, pathways to history that he'd look into if he only had the time. He found the past fascinating, but unfortunately, having left his factory to be managed by his brother, Tom, Best had been filling his days with jobs for Nathaniel.

He looked at the pub sign that hung askew and recalled how the paint used to be so vibrant, the crest of arms a gleaming silver, the crossing swords crimson, their handles gold. Now the hues had watered down significantly, pasty greys and beiges, the weather leaving its mark like it had on the building itself. Nathaniel would be doing it up at some point, so he'd said, but he didn't appear to be in any rush, preferring to use it as a meeting spot.

Best dipped beside the pub and unlocked the yard at the back, then, using another key, let himself inside and looked down the corridor through a doorway, beyond which stood double front doors, the glass coated in a layer of grime. He shut the door and went behind the bar, heading for the hatch where the flap was always in the up position, leaning against the wall. He placed his carrier bag on the table in the corner and took out a six-pack of beer, opened one, and settled in to wait.

Halfway down his can, he spotted shadows flickering on the sun-lit wall beneath the hem of curtains close by. It was probably Nathaniel and Karen going past. He took a deep breath, the air scented with stale beer that must have soaked into the carpet, and dust. The years of neglect and the remnants of the flood were plain to see, everything so tired and worn out. A newspaper lay on the carpet in front of an ancient slot machine, and it was obvious *The Guardian* been soaked and had dried out into undulating shapes like the moors he'd travelled over to get to Nan and Granddad's.

It made him want to visit them, to turn back time and go to their town by Manchester, but they didn't live there anymore. Didn't live anywhere except under the earth. He'd encouraged them down to London, setting them up in a ground-floor flat. Then Granddad had died, and Nan had followed shortly after, leaving Best full up to the top with guilt that he couldn't shift even now. He tormented himself that if he'd left them alone up north they'd still be alive today. It didn't matter that they'd had underlying health issues they hadn't told anyone about, he carried the burden of their deaths as if he'd instigated them.

He'd been tempted to visit old Beatrice this morning, but Nathaniel said he'd do it, and besides, Best would only be going there to get a 'nan fix', where he'd hand her flowers and chocolates and make her a cup of tea, sitting at her dining room table, talking while they drank a whole pot.

He scanned the area nearest to him and sighed at the peeling wallpaper which had been put up at a more prosperous time, yet years later it looked nothing like it would have done in its heyday. Best had seen pictures of the Galway online, amazed at how beautiful it had been compared to now.

A clatter from the corridor drew his attention that way, and he sat upright, his hand going straight into his jacket pocket, curling his fingers around the handle of his small gun.

"Do you think anyone saw us from over the road?" Karen said.

"So what if they did? I own the fucking place."

"But we don't usually come here together in the daytime. Because of the note, I'm worried that someone saw us coming in here and they were earwigging when we were talking about Paddy."

"We've got no choice but to come here. If you're at my flat, that will get noticed even more, and I don't trust that there aren't cameras in Dad's house that I'm not aware of."

They appeared behind the bar, and Nathaniel looked directly at Best as if he knew damn well where he'd be.

"Shit," Karen said to him, a hand on her chest, "you frightened me, sitting there."

Here we go. She's going to have a little fit because I heard what she was saying. She'll get paranoid and panic.

Best was convinced she'd go off on one any second, but she didn't. She rushed over to the table, pulling one of the cans off the plastic rings and opening it, taking a long swallow. Bloody hell, she must have needed that. She sat on a burgundy velvet stool, her breathing heavy.

"Thank God you're here," she said to Best. "I take it you're going to be the one waiting when they come to collect the money."

Best frowned.

Nathaniel tutted. "He doesn't know what we're here for yet." He came over and sat on a chair that had leather on the seat, cracked and split from being soaked in floodwater, the yellowing foam beneath poking out. A disgusting scent of mildew puffed up, and he grimaced, reaching over for a wooden chair instead. He sat again and took a deep breath, telling Best who had been in the smelter last night and why—but also that Nathan or Karen hadn't had the chance to kill Paddy, someone else had.

Best had a feeling Nathaniel hadn't wanted to tell him that information, but it was obvious they needed some help here.

"I need you to do some digging about who'd want Paddy dead and whether there are rumours that I was the one meeting him at the warehouse," Nathaniel said.

Best shook his head. It was like Nathaniel didn't know how things worked for someone like him. "I'm going to have to be careful, I can't outright ask questions, not in the Bell."

"That's not what I want you to do," Nathaniel said. "You just need to listen, see what you pick up. I don't want anyone to actually know we're looking for them."

"Why not?"

"Karen got a note early this morning." Nathaniel took his phone out and showed Best a picture of it.

Best now understood why Karen had needed that beer. She must have been shitting herself ever since she'd read the words. "Oh. So someone's found out what you were up to regarding Paddy. Is that why I'm here, because you think it's me?"

"Fuck, no." Nathaniel put his phone in his pocket. "You're here because it's like Karen said, I want you to watch while they come to collect the money."

"You can bet they'll be keeping an eye on this place by tonight and will see me turn up later."

"That's why you'll be staying here from now until then."

Best was about to have a right old gripe but thought better of it. Staying in this manky place on his own would be boring as fuck, but Nathaniel wasn't the sort of person he could say no to. The leader's son had too much on Best, who had no choice but to do as he was told. "What about my lunch and dinner?"

"Karen made you some sandwiches. They're in a bag in the corridor as well as some tea in a thermos and some crisps, snacks, and whatnot."

"What's the whatnot?"

Nathaniel smiled. "Black tracksuit, balaclava, a gun."

"I've got my own shooter."

"Then I'll take the other one back with me. I wasn't sure if you'd have bought yours, see."

"I'll need my van; I walked here. Things might get messy, so I'll need the hose, and maybe even the fireworks." Best handed his keys over to Nathaniel.

"I'll get someone to leave it out the back later and make sure the number plates are changed."

"Thanks."

Best thought about the amount of hours he was going to have to sit here. It stank, it was cloying with the smell of mould and mildew, the type that would cling to his clothes and skin, staying up his nose for days afterwards, but he'd get paid a lot of money for this, so it was a case of shrugging and getting on with it.

Nathaniel went through the plan, and Best held back a frown, thinking about the weight of what they intended to do. He worried about

Karen. Could she handle this? He didn't dare voice his concerns, Nathaniel probably wouldn't appreciate it, not to mention the woman herself getting offended. She'd likely accuse him of thinking of her as a damsel in distress and spout some feminist quotes at him.

"I put a book in the bag," she said. "You said once you like to read but didn't have much time."

He not only appreciated the thought but the fact that she'd even remembered something like that. No wonder Nathaniel was knocking about with her behind his old man's back if she was the thoughtful type. You didn't get many of those to the pound.

They discussed the plan for another hour, going over and over it until it was drilled into Best's head. Karen had mentioned two people in a Fiesta—one had posted the note, the other had driven him away, although she hadn't seen who that was, nor much of the poster because they'd had a hood up, but she reckoned it was a man, going by the build. If Best hadn't killed Rob, he'd have sworn blind it was the Carter brothers pulling a fast one.

But where would the Carters have overheard any discussion regarding Paddy's imminent murder? Or had it been a case of Paddy talking about going to the warehouses to meet Nathaniel? That was more likely, he'd been a blabbermouth, and Best said as much now.

Karen laid a hand on her chest. "Oh God, that's made me feel so much better. I was paranoid that Henry had been listening in at the house, hidden devices and whatever."

"I assume you don't get up to anything together while in that house," Best said. "Henry's bound to have cameras, not just listening devices."

"We're not stupid," Nathaniel said. "I grew up listening to my father talk business, don't forget."

Best glanced at his phone for the time. "Fair enough. You'd better get going before the street fills up with parents and kids coming back from school."

The two stood, and Best followed them out into the corridor, locking the door behind them. He had a root around in the bag, finding a crime book, chuffed Karen had also remembered the title he'd mentioned of the one he'd read if he *did* have the time.

Well, now he did.

He set an alarm for nine-thirty, in case he fell asleep, and parted one of the curtains so he had a wedge of light to read by. He sat out of view of the window, taking the clingfilm off one of the sandwiches. Egg and cucumber, something else Karen had remembered he liked. He wasn't sure whether to feel happy about it or weirded out. She clearly had a good memory and listened to exactly what people said. Was that something he needed to worry about? Did Nathaniel?

He switched his mind away from her, and while he ate, he got lost in the labyrinth of his mind, seeking his granddad out, wishing he could talk to him about the life he'd found himself in. The old man would be in one of his tweed jackets, and he'd have picked a comfy armchair to sit in, not a wooden one. He'd say Best had made decisions that only he could carry the weight of—they were his and his alone. He'd say perhaps it was better to get up and walk out now, to cut ties with Nathaniel, but that wasn't possible. Deaths threaded them together, binding them for life, and Best was the one who'd be in trouble if DNA was found in that smelter, because he owned the bastard factory.

No, he couldn't walk away. His mind groaned under the weight of the secrets he now kept; they woke him at night sometimes.

He no longer wanted to take anything for granted, like tonight's plan going smoothly, so instead of reading, for now he went through all the scenarios of what could go wrong so he'd know what to do if it did. Everything could change with the click of a finger and thumb, but not if he could help it.

Chapter Seven

*D*ear Diary,
   I'd known he was going to, but he died. I just didn't think it was going to be so soon. Didn't think that this morning, Mum's scream would wake me up. I'd always imagined I'd find him, not her, and I'd sink to my knees by the side of his bed,

put my hand on his, and tell him I hated him because he'd left me.

I can't do that now, there are too many people here, but I really want to. Can you imagine what people would think if they heard me, though? They'd say I was a bitch of a daughter for even thinking of myself at a time like this.

After Mum's scream, I'd run down the stairs, knowing exactly what I'd find but not wanting to. It was so strange, like I knew it was me running, but it was as if my body belonged to someone else. I didn't feel my feet touching the stairs either, it was like I floated and weighed nothing. By the time I reached the doorway, all the weight came back, and I felt so heavy that I had to lean on the frame.

She was standing over his bed, his hand in both of hers, saying that he was freezing, so bloody freezing, and that she needed more blankets to warm him up. She was obviously in denial that he'd gone. I remember thinking he must have died not long after we'd gone to sleep if he was that cold.

She didn't look at me, she acted as if I wasn't even there, and maybe for her I wasn't and all she could see was him, and all she could feel was how she was left with the wrong person, like I feel, and that if she'd have had her way it would be me who was dead and not him. She'd muttered something about ringing the nurse, saying he could be brought back to life, but she didn't do any chest compressions or breathe into his mouth, so on a deeper level she'd known that whatever she did, he wouldn't be coming back.

I almost felt sorry for her in that moment.

I went and rang the nurse, and she turned up within ten minutes. I'd stayed at the living room window to wait for her instead of going in Dad's room, because Mum was crying and it was getting on my nerves.

Anyway, after that, other people arrived, and it seemed like every time I went to go in the room to say goodbye, someone else was in there. They were people I didn't know, so I assumed they were from the hospice or the hospital. No one bothered to explain, and it was one of those situations where I thought it was better that I kept any questions to myself. I was a spectator no one else saw. Invisible.

At lunchtime, someone gave me twenty pounds to go to the shop and get some stuff for lunch. I made cups of tea and sandwiches for everyone while Mum sat on the sofa, allowing herself the luxury of tears and a scrunched tissue constantly up by her nose.

One of us has to keep a level head, and it clearly isn't going to be her. She's gone to pieces, that's what someone said, and they added that you'd think she would have held it together more because she has a child.

It's weird that someone's on the same wavelength as me, which means I don't feel so bad for thinking the same thing.

Not once has my mother asked me how I am. No cuddle, nothing, not even after I asked her about <u>her</u> feelings, you know, to remind her that she ought to be doing the same for her daughter, but no, Julie

Livingstone only cares about herself and what she wants.

People say I'm just like her.

It was ages before they took Dad away. It was after everyone had finished sandwiches, I know that, because I was washing the plates at the sink when someone else arrived with one of those trolley bed things. I didn't turn to watch them take him through the hallway and out of the house, just kept scrubbing the already clean plate. I bit the inside of my cheek, and it was bleeding.

I haven't cried yet.

Mum's gone to bed now. She had to have a sleeping tablet. The nurse said it would knock her out all night, and that was a good thing because she needed her rest, apparently. I'm sitting in my room, the house silent, thank God, because earlier it felt too full and noisy. Everything has kind of lost its colour now, that's the only way I can describe it.

I'm not sure I'm ever going to laugh again.

I've got a photo of me and Dad from last year when we went on a picnic. He'd taken his fishing rod, and I sat on a blanket reading my book. Mum hadn't come, she said she felt sick, but it was more like she didn't want to get her high heels dirty, and she'd probably be bored anyway. Dad had asked someone to take the picture of us; he'd still used his camera from the nineties. It's one of those that connects to the computer by a wire, and he printed the photo on paper, cut it out, then laminated it at work.

I've propped it up on my bedside table, although I can't look at him at the moment, only myself. I can still remember how I felt that day. Instead of sitting by the river I wanted to be sitting by the beach in a bikini. Instead of having sandwiches wrapped in clingfilm for lunch I wanted a three-course meal in some posh place or other. I'd looked at my trainers and noticed how scabby they were. I've still got them now. I really need a new pair, but it's not as if I can ask for any, is it. Dad didn't have life insurance, and he was the only one who worked. Mum was too precious to, or something.

We've been on benefits ever since he got poorly, and I can't see her going out to work now. Dad treated her like a princess, the same as her dad when she was growing up, so she hasn't got any concept of having to lift a finger other than to flick a feather duster around and hoover every now and then. She made housework a game ever since I was little, basically teaching me how to do it for her.

If I stay here with her, I'm going to become the skivvy while she sits and cries on the sofa all day. I can't fucking stand it. I need to get out of here, find a better life, but there's school to finish first.

I'm going to try and get some sleep, but it might be hard because there's no sleeping pill for me.

Love from,
Karen Marie Livingstone

The nip in the air gnawed at Karen's cheeks. It was October, two weeks after Dad had died, and the cold outside was just as brutal as the cold that had settled in her bones this past fortnight. The heating hadn't helped to thaw her, nor had the thick black coat she'd borrowed from Mum. It was the type of cold that couldn't be warmed up.

She reckoned she'd be freezing forever, couldn't imagine ever being a normal person again.

She was empty, grief hollowing her out, mainly because she had to endure it alone. Mum was next to useless—her new husband was the bottle now, and he went to bed with her every night. He kept her company during the day like she'd done for Dad, and she talked to Mr Vodka about the past and how things weren't supposed to turn out like this.

Karen stood beside the grave the coffin had just been lowered into. People huddled around her, stealing warmth from arms touching arms, and she had to move away several times to break contact. The priest had finished talking, Mum had thrown a flower into the hole, and now everybody chattered, albeit their voices low. Karen wasn't listening, their words were just a constant hum in the background of her thoughts that were screaming that she had to get away from here, away from that fucking hole that held the most precious person in the world to her.

She stared at the lid of the coffin with its scattering of mud and a single white rose. Mum had got some benefit or other to help her with the funeral cost, and it seemed such a shame that the beautiful, shiny wood wouldn't protect Dad from the worms and spiders and ants.

A harsh wind sifted through the bare branches of a few trees and rattled over the leaves of others. She imagined the branches as skeletal limbs, much like Dad would look one day when his flesh had rotted. She couldn't stop thinking about that, how she'd have preferred him to be burned, because burying someone, wasn't it prolonging grief when you got upset that horrible things were still happening to the body years down the line? That wasn't laying someone to rest, and it certainly hadn't given Karen any measure of peace. Every day she'd wonder when the first insect had got inside that coffin, and then other thoughts would follow, until she saw the coffin jam-packed with a writhing black mass, bugs crawling into his ears and under his eyelids, in his mouth. Or were all of his holes blocked up before he was put in there?

Her subconscious must have picked up on the fact that everyone was leaving, and with her head still down she followed the crowd towards the car park where she'd probably have to thank them for coming, whoever the hell some of them were, and then she'd wait with Mum until they'd all disappeared so no one knew they'd had to get the bus here. The benefit loan hadn't stretched to them having a special car that followed the hearse.

If Karen ever had a husband, she'd make sure there were all the bells and whistles at his funeral. There would be a wake, too, with lots of food and drink, not just a quick knees-up down the local pub where you bought your own drink and a packet of salt and vinegar crisps. She wanted so much more than what she had, and she was determined to get it.

Chapter Eight

George and Greg stood in the back room of The Eagle. Nathaniel sat at the old card table, clearly agitated at not being on his own turf. But that was tough. If he wanted the twins helping to get rid of his father, then things had to be on George and Greg's terms. That was what some leaders failed to understand, that you could do what the fuck you wanted on your own manor, but when you wanted another leader's help then you owed it to them to do as you were told regarding their rules.

I think he's got the gist now, although he looks a bit of a sulky bastard still.

The scent of beer from the bar seemed to coat the walls in here, as did the tang of cigarette smoke from years gone by, and cigars like their father, Ron, had chuffed on while gambling his evenings away—or more like swindling players out of their hard-earned cash, the bastard, then forcing himself on women afterwards.

Jack, the landlord, had already been in with drinks, and his wife, Fiona, was dishing up her chilli. Greg seemed to find the middle distance interesting, while George stared at his shoes which could do with a clean. He'd forgotten to change out of them when he'd taken their dog, Ralph, for a walk in the field behind their house, and he hadn't changed them afterwards either.

The occasional clink of glasses came from the pub, interspersed with chatter and laughter, and if they had more time he'd stop in to have a chat with the customers, but as usual, being social was limited.

A tap on the door announced Fiona, who came in with an extra-wide tray and placed the bowls of chilli and plates of garlic bread on the table. She raised a hand at Greg's thanks, leaving them to it.

George sat, Greg following suit.

"Eat." George gestured for Nathaniel to take a bowl and spoon.

Nathaniel glanced around as if he thought people stood in the darkened corners, listening for what they were about to discuss. Fair enough, this pub was new ground to him, and for all he knew there could be listening devices set up.

"Don't be worried," Greg said. "If we didn't trust Jack and Fiona, we wouldn't have suggested having our meeting here. You don't have to worry about us either. We're here to discuss your father, nothing funny going on."

Nathaniel adjusted the sunglasses he still had on, perhaps his safety blanket, but George didn't like not seeing the man's eyes. He reached over and took them off the bloke, placing them on the table.

"We went to see your old man," he started. "He told us everything we need to know to have an excuse to kill him. If you ever tell anyone, other than Karen, what's going on here, then we will maim you, paralyse you so you spend the rest of your life in a wheelchair, and cut out your tongue, and after that we'll take over your Estate."

"I swear to God, I just want my dad gone. He's an utter bastard. The things he did to me as a kid…"

George's interest piqued. "Hang on a minute… You said the things he did to you as a kid… Was he a fucking nonce?"

"He watched while his friends…did things. Karen's been through similar. She was raped by the Carter brothers, not that you'll know who they are, while my father sat there and… You get the picture. He paid them after."

"Have you dealt with the Carters?"

"One of them, last night. Well, someone I trust got rid of him. I was busy somewhere else."

"Doing what?"

"It's a long story."

"Just get on with it."

By the time Nathaniel had finished, George had the proper measure of the man. He was in love with Karen and wanted to save her. Karen's logic was that this Paddy character was no better than Henry, someone who used women sexually, touched them inappropriately, and her reasoning was that to save any more women from being upset regarding wandering hands, the bloke had to die.

Except someone had got there first and was now blackmailing them for twenty grand.

To say Nathaniel was in a sticky spot was an understatement, but it sounded like he had everything in hand with the help of a bloke called Shaun Best who currently waited in the Galway Arms, possibly bored out of his skull, until the time came for him to catch whoever it was collecting the money.

"I can understand why you didn't bring Karen here, but we'll need to see her at some point to hammer it home that if she fucks us over then she's dead, but in the meantime, you can tell her."

"She's a good woman. I'll vouch for her. What are you going to do about my dad?"

"You get yourself an alibi by going down the Bell for a few jars, and we'll go to the house and take him away."

"There are cameras."

"I don't doubt it, but we don't intend on going anywhere near the place without our faces covered. Afterwards, we'll send a message to the other leaders that we need a meeting tomorrow morning. You'll need to be there. You'll tell them what you told us about your childhood, and that will be the end of it, the Greaves Estate is yours. You'll go along with what I say: that you confessed to us, here, today, and I blew a gasket and killed Henry tonight."

"Thank you."

George poked his fork in the air towards Nathaniel. "Just remember which side your bread's buttered. Which reminds me..." He picked up a slice of garlic bread and dipped it into his chilli. It wasn't tiger bread in a chicken and mushroom Pot Noodle, but it would do.

Greg had already eaten his while he'd been listening to the conversation, and he now drank his Coke, leaning back, his face in shadow. "We don't like men who hurt kids."

"I didn't much like *being* hurt," Nathaniel said. "But I'm hoping that with him dead it won't...won't be as upsetting anymore."

"There were rumours that your mother got killed by him," Greg said.

George shook his head. "Fucking shocking if it was because he was bored, like Henry implied."

"It happened when I was seven. Once she was gone, that was when the abuse started."

"Do you think she protected you from it before?" Greg asked.

Nathaniel nodded. "She must have done, because it was literally a day or two after she died when he came into my room at night."

George didn't even want to envisage it, or to imagine the fear of a little kid in that situation, his father's friends coming into his private space, and the one man who was supposed to protect him just stood there and watched. "Do you know who the friends were?"

"They're dead."

"Did you do it yourself?"

"Yes, both on the same night."

The pink neon lights of the club down the road fluttered through the thick fog. The two men ahead weaved down the street, drunk from their time in the Queen's Head. Nathaniel had watched them for most of the evening, his face itching from the fake beard, his head hot beneath the beanie hat.

His heart raging, his mind filled with memories.

When he'd seen them for the first time since he'd been a child, all of the old feelings had come back—fear, anxiety, the pain—but now he was an adult, only anger filled him and the need to bring about justice. It pissed him off that they acted as though they didn't have a care in the world, like they hadn't abused a little boy—and maybe other children—for years.

Clearly, men like them didn't have a conscience. Was it possible that they didn't think they'd done anything wrong? Yes, they likely knew that abusing children wasn't right, but some people didn't care about the law or the feelings of the people they were hurting. So long as they got what they wanted, then that was okay.

The scent of the wet tarmac was heavy, as was the cigarette smoke from one of the men holding a fag. Laughter came from behind, people likely coming out of the Queen's Head, but with the fog as his friend, Nathaniel wasn't bothered about being seen. His abusers presented as murky, fuzzy shadows, even though he was only two metres behind them, so whoever had come out of the pub probably couldn't even see him at all. He was a ghost in the mist, his plan *to commit murder thought about on many nights in the past couple of weeks. He was a predator, his twisted sense of purpose shunting him forward despite him knowing that what he was about to do was illegal. But then weren't all the murders he'd committed illegal? He couldn't bring himself to admit that taking the law into his own hands was a bad thing to do, because sometimes it was a good thing to hurt bad people if it meant those people couldn't hurt someone else.*

Preventative measures.

To get a feel for them, he'd been following them in a stolen car, or, like tonight, on foot. The easy way they had about themselves infuriated him. He hated how carefree they were, how their actions hadn't affected them in the slightest, yet they continued to live rent-free inside Nathaniel's head, wreaking havoc.

They turned a corner, Nathaniel losing sight of them, so he hurried on, cursing when one of his feet scuffed the pavement. He went left. The fog had cleared in patches, revealing snippets of houses and cars, and someone in this long street was going to wake up in the morning and find bodies. Or maybe someone coming from the club or the pub would literally stumble over them within the hour. Nathaniel didn't care so long as he wasn't anywhere near the area when it happened.

Like the neon sign, one of the streetlights flickered, and for a few seconds, darkness closed in around them. Then the light was back on, and they walked into a cloud of fog. Nathaniel grabbed the opportunity to get the job done. He took a gun out of his coat pocket, walked even faster so he was a stone's throw from the men, then he raised the weapon and prayed the silencer prevented too much noise. He shot them in the backs of their heads in quick succession, then ran off, his footsteps echoing. He almost smacked into a lamppost at one point but veered at the last second.

He took a right onto a cobblestone street. The moisture clung to his face and got into his lungs. Voices came from somewhere, an argument between a man and a woman, the words indistinct as though the fog had smothered them.

Soon he slowed, reaching the deserted road where he'd left the stolen car. He drove to a lay-by and set the vehicle on fire, jogging to his flat after. Even if he got nicked for this, it would be worth it.

"Who found them?" George asked.

"Some poor cow going out about half one before her shift at the hospital."

"Did your dad ever wonder whether you were involved?"

Nathaniel shrugged. "He never said. I was going to bring up the fact that they were dead, but if I did then it would be obvious I had something to do with it. He went to their funerals, though."

"It would look weird if he hadn't." George slapped his palms on the table, his chilli bowl jumping up then clattering back down. "Any preferences on the manner of death?"

"No, I just need him dead."

"Do you want his body put anywhere or hidden?"

"Put him on display. Naked."

"The police are going to view the footage at the house, so leave the cameras pointing exactly where they already are in case they want to look at previous days. They'll spot it immediately if they've been moved on the day of the murder."

"I don't plan to go back to his house again today anyway. What do we do about Karen?"

"We should be in and out without her waking up."

"He'll be a dead weight—she usually drugs him before bed."

"That could show up on tox screens, even if she doesn't do it this evening. What is she giving him?"

"Sleeping tablets."

"And where is she going to say they've come from?"

"I'll talk to her."

George stood. "We need to be getting off."

He walked Nathaniel out the back and shook his hand. "Go and get ready for your evening down the Bell."

Chapter Nine

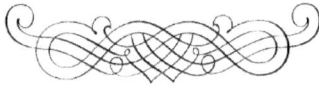

B est had read three-quarters of the book by the time he had to close it. The light from outside had all but gone, and the nearest streetlamp was too far away to cast any significant glow through the window. He should use his torch on the phone, but he didn't want to risk anyone seeing the light inside, even though he'd just closed the gap in the curtains. He placed the book on the table and stretched his arms upwards to give his muscles a small workout.

It was about time he thought about changing his clothing, switching his outfit to the black one that had been provided. The 'whatnot'. He stuffed his own outfit in the bag and would change into it at the factory later. The gun he placed on the table.

As his phone clock clicked over to just before ten, he peered out from the edge of the curtain into the street. The houses opposite stood in darkness. A figure approached the pub; it presented as a silhouette and moved with stealth, as if they were poised to run at any moment. Someone should have been staking the pub out all evening, watching for Nathaniel to turn up, but going by this clown, this was his first time down here today. He wasn't a resident, that much was obvious. With a balaclava covering his face, he glanced back as if waiting for somebody else to follow—or checking if he was being followed—then disappeared down the side of the pub.

Best's stomach did that little flutter it always did just before a job. He picked up the gun.

Walked over to the hatch and braced himself against the wall, cloaked by a thick wedge of shadow created by the shelving unit above the bar. He stuffed his phone in his tracksuit bottoms pocket but kept his hand on it. More than ever he was aware of how much the scent of stale beer was prevalent here. Furniture seemed to loom out of the darkness, unnerving him.

The click of the yard gate was faint. Best and Nathaniel used a key to unlock it, so whoever this person was, did they know there was a lock and they'd come prepared with a pick? Or did they generally carry a pick on them for this kind of eventuality? Best was inclined to go with the former—he reckoned this place had been chosen for a reason: because the person had been here before. They must have done to have known there were beer kegs in the yard, which they'd mentioned in the note.

Best slipped behind the bar, adrenaline racing through him. He pressed himself to the wall going down the corridor, then nipped across into what had once been an office, the summer sky giving enough light for him to see. It was like one big memory, a dusty one at that, the desk covered in a thick layer, papers spread in a fan, a file with its cover curled. Even an old mug, the contents long gone through evaporation, although a dirty brown circle stain remained where tea or coffee had once been. Debris littered the floor, and he had to step his way over it, mindful of a broken wine bottle.

The windows weren't as grimy as at the front, and he was able to see into the yard—which meant the visitor might be able to see him, although the view was a little hazy. Someone was out there rummaging behind the metal beer kegs. Whoever it was froze, as though they knew they were being watched, then they resumed looking for the money, which wasn't there. Well, they'd find a bag if they kept searching, but it would have paper inside, cut up to the size of ten-pound notes.

While the person was busy, Best studied the yard, coupling what he could see with what he remembered of it in his head. A crumbling brick wall stood opposite, beside the gate, graffiti on the other side, most likely created by kids who had a lot to say but found no one was listening at home. He could imagine what it had been like back in the day, the yard busy at delivery time, the barrels being rolled down the hatch into the cellar.

Concentrate!

He shouldn't be letting his imagination run riot.

Movement caught his attention to the right. Fuck, someone else was in the yard, standing beside some old-fashioned metal rubbish bins. They lifted one of the lids. The other person spun round at the sound of the scrape and clang of metal. That's when Best got a good look at a face. The one after the money behind the kegs was Oscar, he'd rolled his balaclava up to his forehead. This was the perfect opportunity to kill the little bastard, but it meant also killing his companion who had their face covered with a bandana, only their eyes visible and surrounded by a close-fitting hood.

Best ground his teeth and racked his brain on what to do.

Sometimes Oscar hated it when people found things out before he did, but in this instance, being told that there was an opportunity to make some serious money had overridden any irritation he'd felt.

He normally did this kind of job with his brother, but Rob was being a prick and not answering his phone or the door to his gaff, so he was going to miss out on sharing the spoils. Ten grand was a lot, and Rob was going to kick himself when he found out about this. Still, Oscar would tell him it was a lesson learned.

He hadn't expected to bring someone else with him tonight, he'd been prepared to do the collection alone, but they'd insisted, seeing as though they'd been the one to overhear the information about Paddy Winchester meeting Nathaniel at the warehouses; they'd also suggested Oscar murder Paddy and demand twenty grand.

Oscar had stabbed Paddy while his companion had kept watch, and then they'd gone off to celebrate, high on the adrenaline of a kill, and a few hours later he'd posted the note at Henry's house. He'd made sure his face wouldn't be caught on the camera above the front door.

He continued to root around for the money. Where the fuck was it?

Frustrated that he wouldn't be able to open the window because it would make too much noise, or even, going by the thickness of the paint, it wouldn't open at all, Best was going to have to shoot through the glass. There was no way he was going to let this opportunity slip by. He scanned the yard—Oscar still nosed about for the money, but the other one had retreated to the corner by the gate and blended with the darkness to the point that Best struggled to see them properly. Once the window had been shot out he'd have a clearer view, but he was going to have to shoot Oscar and then fire into the darkness in quick succession, otherwise the second person could get away, and he wasn't going to let that happen, not again like it had in Rectory outside the old dear's house.

The person in the darkness stepped out and walked towards Oscar. Going by the body shape it was a girl or a young woman, and Best faltered for a second—killing a woman… But did it matter *who* it was? If they were associated with Oscar then they had to be scum.

He lifted the gun and fired at the girl first. The glass shattered. As he'd planned, she fell to the ground so she blocked the gate, impeding Oscar's escape, although Best didn't intend for the man to get away. Oscar stared at the fallen body and then at Best who'd already aimed again. He pulled the trigger. The bullet smacked into Oscar's forehead, the force of it flinging him backwards against the crumbling wall. It sounded like bits of brick had come off, the noise of it hitting the ground a shower of dull tinkles. Oscar slid down the wall, ending up in a slump.

Best left the building to inspect what he'd done and calculate the clean-up and how extensive it would be. The holdall containing the tarpaulin he'd requested sat like a hunched figure beside the pub door, and he climbed onto one of the kegs to look over the wall. His small van had been left there, as promised. There were no houses behind the pub, thank fuck.

Nathaniel had put on a false number plate.

Best got to work, calculating whether the two bodies would fit inside the size of tarpaulin he'd asked for. He took it out, shaking it from its folds and placing it on the ground. It would be big enough.

Was the girl the driver who'd waited for Oscar to deliver the note to Karen? Or had these two been employed by someone else to do it? Wouldn't it be a turn-up if Henry was behind it all?

Best checked inside the holdall for the tape, then went to pick up the first body. He'd hit her in the heart, which meant more blood than he'd like, but the darkness had been against him. He carried her to the tarpaulin and put her on it. Curiosity got the better of him, and he switched on his phone torch, putting it on the low beam. He pulled down her bandana.

Oh fuck.

Despite knowing who she was, he dismissed her for now and collected Oscar, resting the bastard on top of her and then rolled them up, sealing the tarpaulin like a package.

He opened the yard gate and poked his head out. No one was around, so he dragged the body packet out to his van, struggling to put it in the back as they were fucking heavy. He was going to have to clean out here now, the tarpaulin had picked up some blood from the yard and it'd left tracks on the road. He sorted his hose contraption in the back of the van and sluiced the tarmac. The hose didn't reach into the yard, but the spray jetted far enough that it cleaned up the claret by the gate from the female. He was going to have to clean the other part some other way. The pub still had running water, he'd used the toilet several times today, so he'd have to find a bucket.

He stuck the hose away and secured the van, entering the yard and closing the gate. He drew a rusty, stiff bolt across the top, then turned to skirt around the wet patch in the yard — he didn't want to take blood indoors if he could help it.

He found a commercial kitchen and opened a tall cupboard. Cleaning products lined two shelves, the labels old-fashioned, like from the eighties, but he supposed the contents would still do the trick. Did stuff like that go out of date? He grabbed a couple of flagons of bleach, the five-litre type, and went back to the yard, getting on with the job of erasing evidence of a crime.

It was as clean as he was going to get it in the dark. Nathaniel was going to have to come back tomorrow and do an inspection. If it still needed sorting, then he could do it himself.

Best collected his bag and book from inside the pub and locked the building, securing the yard after him and then driving to the factory.

When the job was done, his murder outfit in the smelter with the bodies, and he'd changed into his other clothes, he messaged Nathaniel.

B: SORTED.

N: OKAY, GOODNIGHT.

B: NIGHT.

Chapter Ten

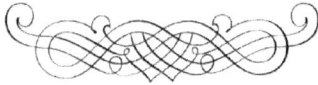

*D*ear Diary,
    I'm not going to say this is shit news because it isn't. Mum's dying. Is it any surprise after the way she's been knocking back the drinks since Dad died? Years of it, of her drowning her liver and preventing me from moving out, laying

the guilt at my doorstep, saying that if I walked out I was a bad person. How can I be a bad person when I've cleaned up her sick where she spewed on the floor and the smell stuck in the carpet? How can I be a bad person to be going out to work because her benefits aren't enough to even feed us both?

What the hell has my life become? During the day I work in an office I can't stand, doing admin, and at night I'm an escort, although I always refuse the extra money for sex. My boss would sack me if she found out I accepted it — "It's not that type of agency, Karen!" — and besides, if sex is always as crap as it was with the two men I've been with, then why would I bother anyway?

The next time I do it I want it to be with someone special — or someone with a lot of money, at least, so the presents he buys me can scrub away the memory of being in his bed.

I plan on being rich, so watch this space.

Lots of love,

Karen Marie Livingstone

The antiseptic smell was the same as the one when Dad was in hospital. Did they all use the same disinfectant or what? Every time Karen took in a breath that was a bit bigger than usual, she smelled it worse, and it reminded her she was sitting where she didn't want to be, on the comfy chair beside her mother's bed, just waiting for her to make the unmistakable sound of a death rattle.

Thousands of people must have died here, and Karen didn't give a shit about a single one of them. There must be something wrong with her; empathy and sympathy were generally things she only directed at herself. When she was the topic, she could feel it all then.

For others, no.

Maybe she was broken.

The machine diligently keeping Mum alive wheezed, and it bleeped every so often. Unfortunately, it hadn't done that long siren it did on the telly when people died, but that would come, hopefully when Karen wasn't here. She wasn't sure whether she'd be able to hide the smile that she was finally free, so it would be best if she avoided that particular situation.

When the nurse had turned the lung machine off earlier (it probably wasn't even called a lung machine, but that's what Karen thought of it as), maybe to see how her patient managed on her own, Mum's breathing had turned shallower, although it was noisy. The nurse had listened for a while, taking the pulse, then nodding and switching the machine back on. Karen didn't understand why they were keeping the woman alive when her liver was absolutely fucked, not to mention her kidneys. It didn't make sense. Why not just switch that machine off permanently and let her slip away?

Maybe they'd do it tonight after Karen had gone home. She'd already said she couldn't stand to be here when her mother passed away — too painful, she'd told them, squeezing out a few tears.

Out of the corner of her eye, she spotted one of the nurses watching her from the station where a couple of others sat in front of computers. Karen pretended she hadn't seen her and reached out to hold Mum's hand, the skin withered as though she was thirty years older than she was. The alcohol had ravaged her on the outside, too. Karen didn't want to hold her hand, but it would be expected of her.

She'd like to say those fingertips had smoothed hair away from her forehead when she'd been poorly, or the palm had cupped her jaw when her mother had looked down at her with love in her eyes, but no such thing had happened. Dad had done it, and Karen cherished those memories, but all this hand had done was apply makeup and rise to allow Mr Vodka to kiss her lips.

Karen let it go and patted it as if she gave a shit.

It had been two days since Mum had last opened her eyes. She usually recognised Karen even when she was pissed up, but the last time Karen had looked into those grey-blue irises, there had been no recognition whatsoever.

Karen got up, kissed Mum's forehead, held back a shudder, and walked out of the ward. Hopefully she'd get a phone call later, or in the middle of the night, saying that she was dead.

That would be nice, wouldn't it.

Chapter Eleven

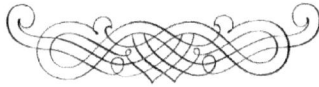

It was nice going to the pub on a summer evening, although Nathaniel wished he was sitting outside at the bench tables where it was cooler. Instead, he was indoors at the Bell, nursing a third pint of Guinness. He'd been seen by a fair few people, some had even come to speak to him, so as far as he was concerned his alibi was watertight. Even better there was a lock-in. Tonight was one of those rare ones where he'd taken time to actually immerse himself in his surroundings and the tapestry of lives that some customers had unpicked before him, revealing parts of their soft bellies usually reserved for loved ones, but he'd always found that people warmed to him rather than his father. Their confessions had taken his mind off what was going on elsewhere.

Despite half of the punters leaving, a lot of laughter filled the pub, glasses tapping on tables as they were placed down, the odd argument breaking out about something or other. A fair few colourful characters had remained, ones who could tell a good story if they'd had enough to drink, getting the whole pub laughing.

Two blokes with rumpled shirts sat nearby, chatting about work, and on Nathaniel's other side, two lads in their twenties, faces bright from the splash of their phone screens. A couple of old men sat by themselves.

The air seemed to get progressively worse, hotter, and someone with red hair whinged about it. The landlord, Vancey, stuck the air-conditioning on, grumbling about the cost of electricity, then further complaining because someone knocked on the front door. He came out from behind the bar and headed towards it. Nathaniel stiffened. What if it was the police? There could be questions about the Carter brothers. Or worse, what had gone down at the Galway Arms.

Vancey took his phone out of his pocket and looked at the screen. Nathaniel squinted to see that far—ah, a camera app. Handy to know he had one of those, although Nathaniel had never seen the camera out the front of the Bell.

"It's all right," Vancey said and opened the door.

Warm air slithered in, a group of people coming in with it, boisterous, but they soon calmed down when Vancey told them to shut up in case the neighbours opposite complained. They must have been on a pub crawl as they were pissed as farts, reminding Nathaniel that he'd never really had that, a chance to let his guard down, because he was a Greaves and someone always wanted to stab him in the back. He couldn't afford to be vulnerable like them. One of the new women asked if she could put on some music, and Vancey refused on account of the noise, even if he kept it low. He didn't fancy losing his licence. No one seemed to care that Nathaniel was who he was, which made a nice change.

He was dying to go to the factory, meet up with Best while Oscar's body burned to nothing, but if he did then his whole point of being here would have been a waste of time. As it was, he was going to get a taxi, deliberately ordering an Uber so there was a record of him having used it. He also wanted to get hold of Karen, but that wouldn't be wise either, despite them having burner phones now that they could toss at the drop of a hat.

Because tonight wasn't only about catching the bastard who'd killed Paddy and had the balls to try and blackmail him and Karen, it was about Henry Greaves taking his last breath.

He worried about Karen. Her exterior spoke of confidence, attractiveness, someone who had it all together, but underneath she was broken, but wasn't everyone? All he wanted to do was make sure she was happy. With Henry gone, she would be.

He turned his attention to the beer pumps. Vancey reckoned they were the finest ales this side of the river, but Nathaniel had yet to sample any. He'd stick to Guinness because he rarely got drunk on it; he wanted his wits about him tonight, obviously.

A man whose untidy hair stood up in all directions approached. Nathaniel had seen him before, speaking to him once to help him fix the problem of an annoying neighbour. Dave had that look about him where he wanted help again, his eyes darting beneath his shaggy eyebrows. Sweat beaded his face, especially his forehead, and he'd undone the top buttons of his light-blue shirt which had wet patches beneath the armpits, the edges a rugged coastline that had dried beige.

He sat on the stool beside Nathaniel. "I need you to grant me a wish."

What does he think I am, a fucking genie? "What kind of wish?"

"Have you got any names of some decent escorts?"

Is this some kind of joke? About Karen?

She'd told him all about her life, and he'd felt sorry for her, having to do that for a living, but if she hadn't, then they'd never have met. Fate was a funny thing.

"Can you afford one?" he asked.

Dave frowned. "Afford one? I only want some bird to come to a work do with me next week. She'll get free drinks and dinner, so what more would she want? I don't want none of that how's your father."

"Payment for her time, most likely, but as you don't seem inclined to pay, then I can't help you."

"Tsk. I even asked a few of the neighbours, the ones without husbands, obviously, and they didn't want to know. Who in their right mind turns down free grub and booze? I just don't get it."

Nathaniel didn't have the heart to tell him it was likely his appearance that put the ladies off. "You're going to have to shell out, I'm afraid."

"How much?"

"Anywhere between a grand and five."

"You fucking what?"

"Language," Vancey bollocked.

"Sorry," Dave said, "but blimey, that's a lot of money, that is." He chewed his bottom lip. "I can't not take anyone, they think I've got a wife."

"Say she's ill."

Dave pondered that, shaking his head then drinking his beer. Nathaniel took it as his cue to order a taxi, so he went outside with a couple of men who wanted a smoke. He kept them talking until the taxi arrived, so someone had seen him every step of the way, and then he was going to have to do what he'd vowed he would never do again once he'd met Karen, and that was to spend some time with one of the escorts he'd used before he'd met her. He sent a message to Bunny, who he'd been with before, and got the driver to take him to one of his father's clubs, Intoxication, where he made sure to look directly at the camera above the door as he walked in.

The redheaded Bunny waited for him by the cloakroom entrance, legs for miles and a figure to die for, but she'd gone understated and chosen a nice black dress. He slipped her an envelope with cash in which she put in her bag, and they entered the main club. Strobe lights flickered a range of colours over the dancing crowd. The beat rumbled through Nathaniel's body, and once again he was reminded of the fact that he hadn't let his guard down in a club either. His skin seemed to pulse with the music, the energy here frantic, drinks spilling, no one caring.

He guided Bunny to the bar and was seen to straight away by a barman with blue hair and muscles on muscles. He took their order, making their cocktails, showing off by shaking the shaker above his head and then spinning it behind him from one hand to the other. He poured the concoction into two glasses over crushed ice, jabbing in straws and mini umbrellas. Nathaniel took forty quid out of his pocket and handed it over, mouthing for him to keep the change.

They found seats in the busiest part. Nathaniel had told Bunny he just wanted company, she didn't even have to chat, and she definitely didn't have to have sex with him. She wouldn't care what she did, she'd get paid the full whack regardless, and he'd give her a bonus for staying with him until lunchtime. He'd take her to breakfast, again getting seen, and then Karen would phone him to announce that his father had gone missing.

It looked like an argument had broken out between two beefy blokes, both of them pointing at each other, expressions showing anger on one and surprise on the other. The one with the beard shoved the blond, who landed on a table. The people sitting there jumped up to get out of the way, their drinks crashing to the floor. A crowd surged forward to watch, some of them baying for blood and others appearing wary, then the bouncer jumped in from nowhere and wrenched the fighting men apart. He pointed towards Nathaniel, who raised his eyebrows at the offenders, shaking his head and letting them know he'd seen everything.

Two security men materialised, but Nathaniel raised a hand and wagged his finger to convey that he wanted the men to go their separate ways without any retribution. The last thing he needed tonight was for people who'd been here to be questioned and he was linked to letting the staff take the blokes away for a beating. He received frowns in return but didn't care. Everyone dispersed and got on with their evening, Nathaniel watching, Bunny chatting to some woman at the next table about makeup.

He was bored shitless, but this had to be done. When you wanted your father killed, you had to make sure you were clean as a whistle.

The yellow neon light for Intoxication turned the bricks it was attached to a sickly curry colour. It was a relief to be out of the club and on the slick pavement, although it wasn't so good under the sheets of rain pelting down and cooling the summer night. How quickly it had changed, because thirty seconds ago when they'd stepped out of the club, the rain had been falling gently with barely any warning of what was to come. Thunder rolled in the distance, and he looked up to wait for the lightning which never came. The rain drummed on nearby taxi roofs, drowning out the shrieks of women who rushed around like blue-arsed flies in an attempt to not get wet.

Bunny stood beside Nathaniel with her coat over her head. He, on the other hand, let himself get drenched. They were in the taxi queue, and despite who he was, he wasn't going to jump to the front. The scent of petrichor lingered, as did that unmistakable smell of wet tarmac and damp hair. A couple of women fucked about, dancing in the quickly forming puddles, while others complained they were getting splashed.

The rain stopped as though a tap had been switched off, and then came the moans and groans about ruined hairstyles and soaked clothes. Bunny glanced at him from beneath her coat and smiled, her hair dry, her makeup still pristine.

"I'll order us food when we get back," he said.

She nodded. "I got a friend to drop an overnight bag round the back of your place. She put it in the bush. I don't want to go for breakfast in this dress and high heels."

"I don't blame you."

It was their turn to get in the taxi, the driver whinging about his fabric seats getting wet. Nathaniel didn't care. He had an absolutely amazing alibi so far, and he reckoned he'd be golden.

Chapter Twelve

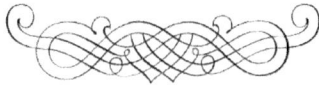

Karen hadn't slept a wink so far. She'd opted to go in the spare room and would tell the police that was a normal occurrence because Henry snored. With him asleep in their bedroom and no word from Nathaniel, she had no clue what had been going on at the Galway Arms and whether it had gone smoothly or not. She'd gone to bed shortly after Henry had zonked out, the sun on its way below the horizon but still light enough that she hadn't closed the curtains while she'd tried to read. Now, with the curtains firmly drawn, the only light she had was the glow of a small lamp that kept the darkness at bay.

It had not long pissed it down, the rain drumming on the window so hard she'd convinced herself it was fingers, and then had come the growl of thunder, only the one, but it had scared her silly. She wondered whether Nathaniel had been caught out in it; he'd said that was around about the time he'd be leaving Intoxication. She'd stored his movements in her head, checking the time periodically so she'd know where he was and what he was doing.

She understood why he'd chosen to have Bunny overnight at his flat. The escort wasn't the type to overstep the mark, she'd do whatever he told her to, keeping it platonic, although she *would* be sleeping in his bed. The police would think it was bloody weird if she didn't, given that he planned to tell them she was his girlfriend.

Karen got up for the umpteenth time and went to check on Henry, even though she shouldn't be doing it in case the twins had already broken in and she hadn't heard them. A shaft of light from the landing night light crawled over her husband when she opened the door, and he lay in the same position as he'd been in last time, on his back. She closed the door to, switching off the night light, returning to the spare room and getting settled again.

Would a break-in be more plausible if her light was off, too? Or would men intent on stealing her husband in the middle of the night not give a shit about that? She had to look at this from the police's point of view and how they'd see it.

She switched the lamp off.

She wasn't sure whether she drifted off or not, but a crack splintered through the quiet, her heart beating ten to the dozen even though she was expecting someone to come into the house. She sat up, a hand to her chest, straining to hear more sounds. Goosebumps popped up on her skin, and she rubbed her arms to make them go away. This house, that she had loved when she'd first seen it, her gold-digger's eyes desperate to take everything in, had now become a prison cell, one she was allowed to leave, yet at the same time she still felt caged when she wasn't in it. It was no different now; she was stuck here while whatever happened played out.

The splintering sound came again. It was like a bottle being broken halfway down the street, faint yet close at the same time. Were they breaking the kitchen window or the one in the dining room? The darkness seemed to hum around her, breathing on her; the fan was doing sod all to keep her cool, and she'd forgotten to put the air-con on.

She rose from the bed, her breathing shallow, although really she ought to stay put—she was supposed to be asleep. Thankfully, her feet didn't make any noises on the carpet, and she moved to stand at the bedroom door, her ear pressed to it.

Nothing. Total quiet apart from her ragged exhales.

Were they already inside?

She returned to the bed, annoyed with herself for even getting out of it, for breaking the bloody rules. She turned the pillow over to the cool side and lay staring into the darkness.

She jumped at a scraping sound—oh God, it reminded her of the shuffle Henry made when he went to the toilet in the morning, but he wouldn't need to be out on the landing, they had an en suite. Had he heard the splintering noise and got up to investigate? But that didn't make sense, the pills she gave him in the whisky always knocked him out, so she doubted he'd have heard a thing.

The scraping came again, and she realised what it was: the patio doors opening and closing at the back of the house. She'd stupidly allowed herself to become frightened, thinking the scrape was something else, instincts kicking in even though she knew how tonight would play out. She was so tempted to watch the twins on the security app, rewinding it to when they'd approached the house, but any access to the footage would be logged, and if she was supposed to be asleep, how could she have possibly done that?

A loud crash shattered the silence, and she jumped again, a small shout of fear coming out of her. She swore someone stood in the corner of the room, poised to come towards her, and she had to turn on the lamp to prove to herself that her imagination was playing tricks.

The familiar creak of the one floorboard in the hallway downstairs ripped out its giveaway sound. Then footsteps—*thud-thud-thud* in a steady rhythm up the stairs. The darkness came closer, suffocatingly black, and she wanted to scream. Her heart raced at the thought of people being inside her house, and it didn't matter whether they were supposed to be there, it was still oddly disconcerting. Panic floated through her, spreading like a weird creepy blanket under her skin, and she shuddered.

The footsteps went along the landing.

She closed her eyes.

Chapter Thirteen

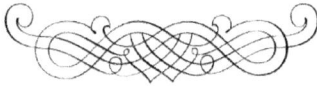

*D*ear Diary,
    I'm going out tonight with a man who doesn't want to be seen in his neck of the woods with an escort, so we're having to go to Essex. I don't mind, the agency are paying for the taxi to take me there, and depending on how it goes

during the evening, I might let the client bring me back to London. Some of them are so super creepy that I just know they're not to be trusted, but others genuinely want a lady to take out for dinner, usually so they can make out to their colleagues that they've actually got a wife.

The amount of times I've pretended to be a wife…

This one needs me to pretend to be his business partner. I've been sent some papers regarding the deal he intends to make, which I've read. The information is simple enough to retain, and hopefully I won't have to do much talking, just look pretty so he can seal whatever needs to be sealed.

Who knows, he might end up being my ticket out of here.

Love from,

Karen Marie Livingstone

Her stomach wouldn't stop churning in the back of the taxi. She'd received a message from the agency to get the cabbie to drop her off at the Pirate's Arms where a *black Lexus would be waiting for her in the car park out the front, registration plate B055Y B0Y. She ran her palms down the skirt of her fitted burgundy dress, touching her hair to make sure the chignon was still in perfect place. This could be it, the night she met her future husband, if Bossy Boy was the type she could manipulate. This could be the start of something big.*

Karen had learned how to impress men, how to come across as someone completely different to who she really was. Tonight she had to be who he needed her to be, someone who reflected the same qualities he had, so they appeared to be a dynamic duo, ready to set the world on fire with their new business, five nightclubs dotted around a section of south London.

Her stomach did another somersault as she caught sight of the pub sign swinging softly. She collected her fake fur coat from the seat beside her and shrugged it on, gripping her clutch bag with its crystals on the front. The fare would have been paid by the agency already, so at least she didn't have to worry about that. The cab drew to a halt, and she stepped out, scanning the car park for the number plate in the darkness. A flash of headlights drew her forward, and she spotted what she needed: B055Y B0Y.

Whenever she met a new client, she had to make sure he matched the photograph in his file. The back window of the Lexus inched down, revealing a man who left her in no doubt he was the one who'd booked her. The passenger door opened at the front, and another man got out, taking her elbow and guiding her around to his side of the car. He opened the rear door and gestured for her to get in, which she did, settling beside Bossy Boy. The door closed.

"For this venture my name is Riley Sanford, and I'm pleased to meet you." He held out a hand for her to shake it, his fingers warm around hers, then he let them go and said, "And you're Miss Rebecca Greene. Riley and Rebecca, R-R, see? We want the backer to think we're the Rolls-Royce of options. Did you read the file?"

Karen nodded as the other man got in the passenger seat and the engine rumbled.

"Good," Riley said.

Riley. She may as well start thinking him of him as that, seeing as that's what she'd be calling him over dinner. The car drew away, and she assessed him without making it too obvious. Could she have sex with him? Could she pretend she liked it just so she could be showered with his money? Not as a client of the agency, but outside it, in real life, so she could give up working in the office, give up being an escort, and live much like her mother had done: makeup, nails, hair…

She'd do anything if it meant she'd live the life of luxury.

The car pulled up outside a glass-fronted restaurant that revealed the diners inside, the light from the many chandeliers glittering off diamond earrings and necklaces, cufflinks, and tie pins. This was a place for the wealthy, and Karen was about to get a big taste of what it would be like to live like this all the time. The place stood out starkly because of the surrounding darkness. Like a pauper, her mouth watering, she stared at someone being served a plate with crabs in their shells on beds of shredded lettuce. She'd only ever had the fake crab sticks from Tesco.

Waiters weaved between the tables, ready to take orders or to deliver food, all of them synchronised, well trained, and so different from what she was used to—a moody cow of a waitress down the pub, chewing bubble gum and making it obvious to everyone she didn't want to be there, working for the minimum wage.

A line of people waited to be allowed in. They hunched inside their coats, gloves on or hands in pockets, scarves tight, clouds puffing out of mouths from hot breaths against the cold evening air. Karen was drawn away from staring—the car door beside her opened, and the man from the passenger seat helped her out. He guided her to Riley who fitted her arm in the crook of his elbow and led her across the road.

They didn't have to join the queue. A man in a suit opened the door, escorting them to a podium where a woman stood, smiling, asking for a name.

"Riley Sanford and Rebecca Greene." Bossy Boy stared at the woman, eyes narrowed.

She ignored his blatant perusal, as if she was so sure of herself, her self-esteem so high that no man would make her feel less than, or ogled, a piece of meat.

Karen wanted to be just like her.

While the woman talked to Riley about tonight's specials, including an apparently good deal on champagne, the price of which was choke-worthy, Karen glanced around to get her bearings. The hushed atmosphere spoke of those who didn't need to be rowdy with alcohol to get their point across. This was a gentle coming together of people who had good breeding, something Karen was going to have to emulate if she wanted the life she had in mind. People would know straight away that she wasn't their kind if she spoke with her usual accent, but she'd been practising being posh in front of the mirror, and she reckoned she'd done really well in disguising her roots.

Tonight was going to be a test of whether she could pull this off for the rest of her life. This was a place where people indulged in elegance. Music played softly in the background, none of this noisy pop stuff down the boozer that got everybody singing when they'd had a few. Here, men wore suits and women gorgeous dresses, the scent of their perfumes and aftershaves creating a big cloud that screamed of expense. White tablecloths reached to the floor, fancy flower arrangements stood on podiums, the walls mirrored on the top half, wood panels on the bottom painted a lovely sage green.

Karen took a deep breath, plastered on a smile, and followed Riley towards their table.

It was showtime.

Chapter Fourteen

George could have screamed in anger when the floorboard had creaked. He hadn't been warned about it, and he'd wondered whether Nathaniel *and* Henry were setting them up. Was the creak of that board *supposed* to occur so Henry just happened to wake up? If George found out they were being played, God fucking help the Greaves men.

The walk along the landing had been fraught with tension, George expecting someone to jump out at him from one of the doorways, each swish of his trainers against the carpet seeming deafeningly loud in the quiet stillness. He'd kept to the shadows by the wall as he approached the bedroom where Henry would be sleeping—or so they'd been told.

Come on, you can handle whatever comes your way.

George paused outside the room and took out his gun in case this *was* an elaborate game and he needed to shoot a motherfucker in the face. He moved slowly, his heart tripping over every beat, and reached out with his left hand for the door handle. He twisted it, pushing the door open inch by inch until the man in the bed was in his line of vision.

A slice of moonlight lit the room, the curtains partially open in the middle. George kept his gun trained on Henry and entered, scanning the shadows for anybody lurking. He got down on his knees, glanced to the doorway to make sure

Greg was keeping watch, then bent to check under the bed. He squinted but found nothing.

He stood again, jumping slightly at movement in his peripheral. The breeze had come through the open window, the curtain shivering, and for one awful moment he thought Nathaniel had been hiding behind it, stepping out to show himself. George's skin had gone sticky with sweat—he was uncomfortable here now, he'd given himself the jitters because of the floorboard, and he wanted out as soon as possible. He couldn't get rid of the feeling that someone was watching. Nathaniel had mentioned cameras. They had balaclavas on, and there was no way they'd reveal their voices by talking, but still, George felt too exposed. Despite the lingering sensation that an unknown presence was nearby—or it could be the knowledge that Karen was in one of the other bedrooms along the landing—he licked his lips, tasting the salt of dried sweat, then moved round to the side of the bed closest to Henry.

He and Greg had discussed this several times prior to entering the property, so there was no need to even tell Greg to play his part. He remained on the landing, ready for if Karen came bursting out, regretting her part in this, while George bent to slap Henry around the face to see if he'd wake up.

Whatever was put in that whisky had knocked him out good and proper.

George lifted him, glad the bloke had pyjamas on so he didn't have to touch any old-man skin, and placed him belly down over his shoulder. He followed Greg along the landing and down the stairs; his brother avoided the floorboard, as did George this time, and they left the house the same way as they'd entered, via the patio doors. Greg used a pick to lock it again, the broken window something to throw the police off and for Colin to use, if he ended up on the investigation, as an avenue to steer the case down: killer breaks window, kidnaps sleeping man, then takes him off to murder him. George wished he'd found some patio keys in the house to make it seem like the killer had used them—it wasn't going to be plausible that he'd carried a sleeping man through a window. Unless he'd pushed him through.

He wasn't going to worry about the logistics, that was Colin's job.

He put Henry in the back of their taxi, lying flat on the seat, and Greg drove them to Cardigan on the quietest streets. After a few loop the loops and lefts and rights, they finally made it to their warehouse. George got out, the night's heat a heavy blanket after the cooler air coming from the blowers in the cab. He was pissed off with sweating all the time.

He carried Henry inside. The warehouse itself was also warm, but when he took him downstairs to the cellar, the air was no longer simmering on a gentle boil. Instead, a shocking and welcome blast of cold hit him; whatever the reason for the change in temperature, maybe because of the stone walls, he was bloody grateful. Goosebumps popped up on his arms, the sweat on his face immediately drying. The scent of the mildewed corners was strong today, not to mention the earthy mineral scent of the stones.

He fucking loved it down here. The chill, how it smelled, how it was so dark until Greg switched the halogens on—all of it turned him from a semi-normal man into a monster, more so when he saw his tools on the table, the whips, electric saws. Whenever he put on a forensic suit—and even when he didn't—that was it, he became the part of himself that he forced to live inside him, in a little pocket of his mind, until it was time to play.

He placed the sleeping Henry on the trapdoor and stripped him naked. Went to use the crank to lower the chains from the ceiling. He clipped the manacles around the old man's wrists, returning to the crank to lift the body. Henry hung there, completely oblivious, until George wafted something under his nose. In the next sharp and sucked-in breath, Henry woke, staring around wildly, panic written all over him, his dick trying to climb inside him to hide with his bollocks. He jerked around, the chains jangling, and then looked at George who stood there with his head cocked, waiting for him to stop being such a fanny.

The chains stilled, and Henry's ragged breathing filled the room. "Wha...? Where...?" He sounded groggy and extremely disorientated.

"You're in our cellar."

"How the fuck did I get here without knowing?" he slurred.

"Your missus has been feeding you sleeping pills every night for a long, long time."

"Wha-aaat?" The bloke was still doped up.

"Nathaniel told us a few stories about you, how you like to watch. I mean, you made it clear enough yourself when you offered to share your wife with us, how you'd sit there and observe, but you said that was her insisting on it. We heard it differently. You like to watch men raping your wife, and you like to watch men raping your son, your little boy who couldn't fight back. Well, he's a big boy now, and he's waited for a fair old while to get you back for what you did."

"Get the fuck out of here," Henry said.

"What, get out of my own cellar? I don't think so."

George had resigned himself to the fact that this kill wasn't going to be much fun. Henry had no fight in him, he had too much whatever-the-fuck floating through his veins; even coming awake and being frightened by hanging from chains hadn't served to give him the dose of adrenaline that would mean he'd be more alert.

Boring fucker.

Still, George put on a forensic suit and gloves, covered his trainers with booties, and pulled the hood up. He selected a cigar cutter, fitting just the tip of one finger into it, watching Henry watching the finger; it was as if the old man thought he was dreaming. George squeezed the handles of the device and smiled at Henry screaming. Greg came down at that moment and stood beside George, grabbing Henry's other hand and bending two of the fingers back. Henry screamed again, and George was naffed off because he couldn't hear the crack of the bones. He dropped the cigar cutters on the floor, grabbing the free hand himself, holding it up close to his ear, and breaking another finger.

He heard *that* crack.

He went over to the crank and lowered Henry until his feet touched the trapdoor. He kicked the back of one knee, and the leg automatically bent, Henry thumping down on his arse.

"I need you to write me a little letter." George told Henry what he wanted it to say. "Think you can manage that?"

"You broke my fingers, and the other one's bleeding, so how?"

"I'm sure you'll manage."

Greg supplied paper on a clipboard, and a pen. He held it for Henry. It took a bit of patience—okay, a lot—for George to remain outwardly calm while Henry fumbled about with the pen using the hand with the fingertip missing, but the letter was done, albeit with his blood on it, and George placed it on the table to dry. Later, he'd fold it up and pop it inside Henry's wallet.

Standing behind Henry, who was too busy weeping over the missing fingertip, George draped the crotch of Henry's pyjama bottoms at the front of the pervert's neck, twisting the leg fabric together until it formed a rope. He used it to strangle, gesturing with his head for Greg to come over and hold Henry's hands down. Greg sat on the bloke's legs, and together they waited the minutes it would take for Henry to choke for air, his lungs giving out on him, his brain eventually dying.

Afterwards, George fed the pyjamas into the log burner and set them on fire, selecting a flick-knife from the tool table, one that was long enough for him to gut Henry when they reached the place where they were going to dump him. Greg unlocked the manacles and picked the body up, George following him up the stairs and going to the store cupboard to get two five-litre bottles of bleach.

With Henry in the back of the taxi, his hand covered by a sandwich bag, they drove to the chosen area, the streets slick with rain. He placed the body facedown on the wet grass, removing the bag from the hand and sticking it in his pocket. Greg screwed the cap off the bleach and started at the head end, tossing the fluid all over the back of the body, George parting the arse cheeks so it even got in there. They flipped him over, and Greg doused him again using the second bottle. George released the blade of his knife and held it out for that to be bleached, too, then Greg stood back out of the way for George to get to work.

He cut a long slice from the base of the ribs right down to the pubic hairs, then cut across as though the stomach was a four-piece pie. He held the knife out again for Greg to wash the blood off it. George put it away and turned to the body. He dug his gloved hands into the open cavity, pulling out as much offal as he could so it spilled over the sides. There was no rhyme or reason to him doing this, just that he wanted it to look like a super-savage bastard had done this to Henry.

Satisfied, George dropped the wallet on the ground. They walked towards the taxi, and George smiled to himself at the thought that if anyone watched them, the whites of their forensic suits would make them look like two ghosts in the night, the stuff made of bad dreams.

Chapter Fifteen

Detective Sergeant Colin Broadly surveyed the crime scene. The pebble border edging the large circle of the communal green glistened, resembling dark, polished jewels beneath a sheen of recent rain. The forensic tent had been put up half an hour ago; they were too late, any evidence on the body had likely been washed away.

He glanced at the sky. Now, it was as if no grey clouds had scudded overhead. The sun had breached the horizon, a honey-coloured glow bleeding into the sky and stretching upwards, tinting the edges of the now-white clouds. Bubbles of rain clung to blades of grass. Things would soon dry out. The day promised to be a hot one again, despite the on-and-off storm during the night which was meant to have cooled everything down and hadn't.

As if just waking up and saying good morning, or perhaps they were complaining at the disturbance, birds twittered, unseen in the trees surrounding the grass. A few wildflowers had opened their petals, turning their faces up in search of the sun. A soft breeze brushed by him, filtering through the leaves that shivered momentarily, knocking off a few of those rain bubbles.

He moaned to himself that he should still be in bed, and he suspected someone else wished they hadn't got up this morning yet, too. The woman who'd made the unsettling discovery currently sat in a police car with a PC, giving her statement. She'd come past the grassy clearing on her bike, caught sight of what she'd thought was a mannequin, and got off to have a closer look.

She probably wished she hadn't.

A café backed onto the grass, its yard, and those of the other shops in the parade, kept private by a long, tall wooden fence. The scent of cakes and bread being baked ready for opening time drifted on the breeze, which was better than the eye-watering smell he'd encountered in the tent.

Colin fancied a blueberry muffin.

He wasn't chuffed at standing here at half past five in the morning, his boss, Nigel, not even here yet, but at least it gave him time to compose himself, wake up a bit. The twins had let him know this body was one of their kills and that it had been dumped on the Cardigan Estate so Colin would hopefully be involved in the investigation, seeing as he was on the murder squad.

Fucking wonderful.

He'd been told the investigation should go in the direction that the dead person had pissed someone off, and that someone had wanted retribution. He'd been taken from his house while he'd slept—he took sleeping pills, apparently, although whether that was George's way of saying they'd drugged the man, Colin didn't know. He'd probably find out later on when he met them at the Taj for dinner, but the tox screen would be available in a few days after the post-mortem, and that would tell the story anyway.

He glanced over at the tent. The murdered man had been exposed to the elements, although how long he'd been there hadn't been confirmed yet. Jim, the pathologist, was in there now doing the preliminaries since the photographer had finished, and he'd likely give some kind of estimation as to the time of death depending on how stiff the corpse was—or not. But the body was a mess, Colin had already been in there and had a quick look, but he'd ducked back out again because of the smell and would return once Nigel had arrived.

A few people came along, a group that were perhaps on their way to work together, their shift likely starting at six. Maybe they'd got off the bus round by the café, but they were being herded away from the cordon by a couple of PCs. The gawkers murmured amongst themselves, clearly shocked and intrigued as to why a tent had been put up, and thank God the front flaps were closed otherwise they'd have had a right eyeful they'd never forget. Their imagination was probably running riot as it was, but seeing things for real would give them nightmares. They'd undoubtedly go off and gossip about this when they got to work, the speculation lasting all day.

A car slowly approached, parking behind a couple of patrol vehicles. Nigel got out but dipped his head back into his car, emerging with a takeaway coffee cup, a can of Pepsi Max, and a bag with a logo on it from the bakery section of the independent petrol station down the road. He gestured for Colin to come over.

"Didn't think you'd have had breakfast," Nigel said, opening the bag and offering first pick of the contents to Colin. He placed the can of cola on the bonnet.

"You beauty, the smell of the stuff baking in that café was doing my head in." Colin chose a chocolate-covered croissant and bit into it, closing his eyes at the buttery taste.

"What have we got?" Nigel asked. "And don't hold back just because I'm eating."

It wasn't lost on Colin that his boss didn't give a shit whether *he* felt queasy talking about blood and guts while *he* was eating. "The man's stomach has been cut open, I think after he'd been placed here, his intestines on display."

"Anything else?"

"He's got no clothes on, but a wallet with identification had been placed next to him, as though they wanted him to be identified."

"Name?"

"Henry Greaves."

Nigel's eyebrows hiked up. "What, *the* Henry Greaves?"

Colin nodded. "The leader of the Greaves Estate, yes." He'd managed to eat half of his croissant so far and now rammed the last half in all at once.

"Wonder why he's been dumped here. Could be a rival thing between leaders, I suppose."

Colin chomped on his food and then swallowed, regretting his haste in eating it now. He should have savoured it, because he doubted he'd have time for lunch later. "There was also a note in the wallet, apparently written by Henry. We'll obviously have to get handwriting analysis done on it, but it's a confession of sorts. There's also streaks of blood on it. It's clear to me he was tortured: some of his fingers are broken, one of them has had the tip cut off, and going by the markings around his neck, he was strangled. I didn't stay in the tent for that long, didn't want to get in Jim's way, plus it stinks in there."

Nigel had finished his pecan Danish and sipped his coffee. "What, of his last meal? Did the intestines split open or something?"

Colin felt sick. "God, change the bloody subject, I've just eaten!"

"Sorry. What did he confess to in the note?"

"Upsetting the wrong person. It's pretty vague."

"No names mentioned?"

"No, just that he deserved what he got—for what, who knows?"

"I hate it when things are cryptic. What time did the tent go up?"

"Just after I got here; SOCO were already on the scene when I arrived. The body got rained on, unfortunately."

Nigel put his cup on the bonnet and took his phone out of his pocket, bringing up a weather app and scrolling across the hourly forecast. What, didn't he believe Colin about the rain? "Yes, you're right, it rained on and off all night. We've been praying for it for days, but I bloody wish it'd held off until after the body had been taken away. Fuck it. A lot of evidence will have been washed off."

Colin was secretly pleased on George and Greg's behalf, but he kept his face straight.

"Do you ever wonder," Nigel went on, "whether if there are really gods up there, they like fucking about with us to see how we react?"

"I hadn't really thought about it. There's something else, but it's probably better if you smell it for yourself." Colin grabbed the Pepsi can and opened it, sipping and trying not to be sick.

Nigel went to his boot and put on a forensic outfit. Colin covered his shoes with fresh booties. He had a good look around again now that the light was getting better. Forensic officers, their uniforms bright compared to the leafy surroundings, dotted the grass outside the tent, looking for clues, meticulous in their attempt to contribute to getting justice for the deceased. Knowing George and Greg and how they worked, the deceased likely didn't deserve justice, but it wasn't something Colin could ever say out loud to his colleagues.

Nigel sipped his coffee. He walked over the grass, approaching the tent. Colin took that as his cue to follow.

EMMY ELLIS

"I'd open the flap for a bit first," Colin suggested.

"Bleach," Nigel said as the air from inside wafted out. "Ah, Jim, you've got the back flaps open, thank goodness."

"It was getting a bit difficult to breathe in here," Jim said.

Colin joined Nigel at the flap and stared in.

"The body's been completely drenched in thin bleach," Jim began. "They even put it in his hair. You can see where it's gone yellowy-orange."

"Looks a frightening shade of ginger to me," Nigel said. "Going by his age, I doubt very much he *chose* to have his hair that colour."

"You never know these days." Jim sighed. "But no, I'm betting the bleach did it. I should imagine he's been cleaned of all evidence, so it's a professional or someone who's researched thoroughly into how to cover their arses when it comes to a dead, naked body. A significant amount of blood would have drained onto the grass and into the mud from him being gutted in situ, but unfortunately, the majority's been washed away or diluted by the downpour. I had a look online and it was quite a lot of rain.

Strangulation is my guess as cause of death, although I won't know that for sure until the post-mortem. He was strung up somewhere, his wrists have bruise rings, he's missing the tip of one finger, and three of them are broken on the other hand. Torture? Now, Colin told me this man's a leader, so all of what happened to him makes perfect sense when you think of how they're rumoured to behave, so…"

"I doubt very much we're going to find anything of significance if it's a leader-to-leader issue," Nigel said. "They'd have covered their tracks too well, but we'll give it a good go, show willing an' all that, but obviously won't be stepping on any gangster toes. I don't fancy a leader putting a target on my back."

"Will we be speaking to them all?" Colin asked.

"Will we fuck," Nigel said. "We'll deal with the twins, or you will. Probably best that police local to each leader helps us out by questioning them. They'll probably be more receptive to their own coppers."

Colin thought he was talking out of his arse, Nigel didn't have the first clue about leaders, only what he'd heard from other officers at the station, so he had no idea that every leader had a policeman in their pocket, and that policeman was likely to be the one to go and speak to them. Nothing was going to get done. Henry Greaves' death would be put down to a gang-related issue, unsolvable, and everyone would move on.

"We'd better go and speak to his wife before I tackle the twins," Colin said. "I rang in for information on that as soon as I knew who he was, and she lives on the Greaves Estate, obviously."

"Now *that* we won't leave to another division. You go and see her, I'll stay here and speak to the woman who found the body. She could be a convenient plant, if you see what I mean, she 'just so happened' to be here this morning. I'll hopefully be able to gauge that during our chat."

"What, you think she was sent to find the body?"

"Hmm."

Colin said his goodbyes and moved over to the cordon where an officer handed him a bag to put his forensic clothing inside. While he undressed, he thought about what he'd have for dinner tonight in the Taj, maybe a nice korma or perhaps something spicy like a jalfrezi. A naan bread would go down well, and a few poppadoms. He might even have half a lager, live a little.

He popped the clothing in the bag, leaving the officer to deal with it, and walked over to a couple of constables chatting to the photographer, waiting for their conversation to finish before he butted in. He recognised one of the lads he got on okay with, Jacob Harding, so he'd nab him.

"Do you fancy coming out with me for the majority of the day?" Colin asked him. "I've got to go and do the death knock first, speak to the wife, see if there are any kids on the scene." He knew there was a son but couldn't exactly say so when that information had come from the twins. "And then unfortunately we're going to have to go and speak to George and Greg Wilkes, which is why I said the majority of the day because we could be driving around for ages trying to find them."

"Rather you than me," the other PC said to Jacob.

Jacob smiled. "I don't mind those two. They're all right if you don't talk to them like they're scum."

Colin wasn't aware of any PCs being in the twins' pocket, but it wouldn't surprise him if Jacob was one of them. Young. Impressionable. Easy to manipulate.

They got in Colin's car. He was conscious he'd been told he wasn't supposed to visit Henry's wife until at least eight a.m. so that the son could get to a café and be seen eating his breakfast—he'd arranged for his father to be killed and needed a super-solid alibi. Maybe—what was her name? Karen, that was it—she'd have a bout of histrionics and they'd have to spend a while calming her down, then he'd encourage her to make Jacob a cuppa and they could waste some time there, even more if he prompted her to talk about her husband in depth.

Much as they wanted to, the twins couldn't control every aspect of an investigation, and if Colin turned up at the freshly minted widow's house an hour too early, then so be it. He was interested to see how she played the game, because she was in on everything with Nathaniel and the twins.

Would Jacob suss it out?

I bloody hope not.

Chapter Sixteen

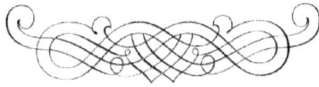

*D*ear Diary.

I've got to claw my way to the top. I'm desperate to get there after all the meals in that posh restaurant. There have been four now, and spending time with Riley, even if it is *pretend, has given me* even more of a taste to be one of the haves instead of a have-nots.

I'm still living in the house I grew up in, for fuck's sake. I had no idea it was a council house until after Mum had died and I'd had to look into paying the mortgage, only to find it wasn't a mortgage but rent. There's nothing wrong with the house now that I'm slowly doing it up, but I want something grander, something people gawp at when they go past in the car.

I'm meant for bigger things.

Tonight's dress is emerald-green velvet, one that Riley sent to me via his driver who came to my house to drop it off after I'd got back from the day job. I could get used to receiving presents like this, especially when they come with a pair of matching shoes that likely cost a month's wages.

Riley's the man I am going to snag. My plan is in action, rather than me just imagining what I need to do to get what I want, what I deserve. The grand house, holidays abroad, the cruises on a personal

yacht, lots of money in my bank account,
enough that I don't have to add things up
in the shop before I put them in my basket.
I'm doing well on my own as I have two
wages coming in, and the agency is cash so
I'm not losing any there to the taxman, but
I want more.

    I want it all.
    Love from,
    Karen Marie Livingstone

Karen and Riley had been sitting in the Mercedes for so long, talking, that patterns of frost decorated the edges of the windscreen. They'd gone out alone tonight, no driver or hardman in the passenger seat. They'd broken down, or so he'd said, and waited for his usual driver to come and pick them up and also arrange to collect the Merc. Personally, because of how long it was taking for anyone to turn up, she had a feeling this had been orchestrated so he could talk to her without her being able to get away.

She'd been with him on several meals since that first time, the pair of them wooing the client, the R-R Rolls-Royce joke wearing thin now, for her anyway, but earlier on, the deal had being finalised, and Riley now had a backer/silent partner for his five nightclubs. He'd told her it was just a front — the real money was in drugs and he needed the clubs as legitimate places to launder the money. Maybe he'd told her that to see if she blabbed, see if he could trust her, but she had securing her own future in mind, so there was no way she'd fuck this man over.

He was about to become the hand that fed her, he just didn't know it yet.

She stared through the windscreen at the grayscale sight before her. This road felt as though it was out in the sticks but did have streetlamps, their glow feeble but better than being in complete darkness. The winter trees, skeletons, reminded her of the ones in the cemetery when her dad had been buried. The branch tips stretched into the black sky, and she shivered, despite Riley giving her a blanket from the back seat to wrap around her shoulders.

"I've got a job for you, off the books," he said. "Nothing to do with the agency. I'd pay you a grand a week for the first part, then fifty grand if you see it through to the end."

She quickly calculated the money. Jesus Christ. "Doing what?"

"Now that's the bit that might make you turn and run."

"Sounds like it's illegal."

"It's very illegal."

"So tell me what it is then."

"Let me just preface this by saying if you don't want to do it, that's the end of it, you never speak about it again—to anyone—and if I find out you have, I'll come for you, and I don't just mean picking you up in my car to take you to dinner, if you see what I mean."

She saw what he meant all right and was intrigued to know what she had to do to earn such a large amount. How far was she prepared to go to get it? *"How long is the grand-a-week stage?"*

"Months. Actually, let's say two years. Less suspicion that way."

Fucking hell, all that cash… *"And the fifty grand?"*

"At the end of the two years."

She was about to ask how he could afford that but then remembered he'd mentioned drugs. *"Why me?"*

"Because you're the only woman I know who'd go for it, who wants the money badly enough."

Shit, had she been that transparent, that greedy? *"What's the final amount for?"*

"Making sure the man you're going to marry dies."

"What the fuck?"

He turned to her, his smile creepy in the semi-darkness. She closed her eyes and turned her head the other way so that when she opened them again she was staring out of the passenger window. The image of the trees along the side of the road would always remind her of this moment, of the seconds before she was going to say yes, even though she didn't know all the details, but first...

"Is my future husband rich?"

"Extremely."

She beamed her own smile at him. "Tell me more."

Chapter Seventeen

The knock on the door shit the life out of Karen. She'd been expecting it at some point, but not this early. It was meant to be at eight. She worried it would be Nathaniel, which wouldn't be unusual, him coming to see his father, something he did every day, but bloody hell, why couldn't he stick to the plan? Or had something gone wrong where it meant he needed to be here now? She hated not knowing all the facts, especially when it involved her husband being killed.

She got out of bed on shaky legs and opened the curtains. The sun was already out, sending its yellow fingers of light over the tropical oasis of the back garden. On days like this she could pretend she was in Spain. It was the kind of morning where she'd usually drink her first coffee out on the patio while Henry still slept, the warmth of the sunrise promising an even hotter day.

She jumped at the second knock on the door. How ironic that she usually looked forward to seeing who was on the other side of it if someone came to visit; it meant she wasn't alone with Henry and the awful way he spoke to her. Guests brought relief, and while *these* guests would undoubtedly do the same, it was in a completely different way to usual. She had to remember not to show that relief when they said her husband was dead.

And he would be, wouldn't he? Surely someone would have got hold of her if things had gone wrong and he was still alive. She was panicking now, her stupid chest going tight from anxiety. To keep herself from spiralling, she concentrated on putting on her lightweight dressing gown, popping her main phone in one pocket and her burner in the other, switched off. She left the room, totally ignoring the one she usually shared with Henry when she walked along the landing, not wanting to see the empty bed he'd been in, not yet. She had to save that so her shock looked more genuine later. She'd planned everything out, her reactions and behaviour.

A third knock at the door had her scurrying downstairs, and it reminded her so much of when her dad had died, Mum's scream still echoing in her ears, that weird weightless feeling happening again where she all but floated. She told herself not to panic and that it wouldn't look suspicious that she hadn't opened up immediately, because it was shit o'clock in the morning and she'd supposedly been asleep with earplugs in. She undid the bolts but kept the chain on, peeking out at the two men on the doorstep, one a young policeman in uniform, the other a scruffy bloke in a suit that looked like he'd slept in it. There was no way his shirt had been ironed.

Mr Tatty held up ID. "Karen Greaves?"

"Yes…" Oh God, it was happening, it was fucking happening.

Maybe they're here to arrest you.

She wanted to be sick.

"I'm Detective Sergeant Colin Broadly, and this is my colleague, PC Jacob Harding. Please could we come in?"

She frowned. "Um, can I ask what for? I don't usually have the police on my doorstep, so as you can imagine, this is a bit worrying."

"I'm afraid we have some bad news. It's about your husband."

She laughed, and it sounded nervous, exactly as she'd wanted it to. "He's in bed, so whatever you want to do him for, you can think again. Come on, come and have a look."

She took the chain off and opened the door wide, gesturing for them to come inside. She tugged at Colin's sleeve, pulling him behind her up the stairs and towards the bedroom, and he protested all the way, saying he didn't need to see the bedroom.

She flung the door open and pointed to the bed without looking at it. "See! He's there."

She stared at Colin.

Colin peered into the room then stared back at her. "Um, the bed's empty."

She glanced from him to the bed, blinking and then gawping at him as if she couldn't believe what she was seeing. "But where's he gone? He never wakes up before nine o'clock. *Never*. He takes sleeping tablets. I saw him take one last night."

"Let's go downstairs so we can talk."

Colin led the way, and Karen launched herself into her role, chasing after him as though she was a panicked wife who didn't understand why her husband wasn't still asleep in bed.

"So what are you doing here? Have you found him wandering around outside or something? Is he in hospital?" She reached the bottom of the stairs, looking at the PC. "I've been worrying that he's got dementia, you know. He's been forgetting a lot of things, getting confused. Is that what's happened? Did he walk out of the house in the night?" She glanced at the front door. "But he can't have done, I had to take the chain off and pull the bolts across just now."

"Perhaps he went out the back?" Colin suggested.

She led the way to the kitchen at first, showing them the back door and that it was still locked. Then she took them into the dining room, indicating the patio doors were also locked. She waved a hand at the window—

"Oh my God! The window's broken!" She slapped a hand to her chest. That was what that splintering sound must have been. She hadn't heard them tapping the glass out of the frame, though, so had it been easy to just take the shards away? The whole pane had gone, giving the illusion that someone had entered the room that way.

"We're going to have to phone for a team to come here," Colin said, "and in the meantime, we'll go into the kitchen because we have something to tell you."

"Okay…" She breathed out through pursed lips. "Okay… He's been hurt, hasn't he. Was he knocked over or something?"

She took them there, going straight for the coffee machine. She needed caffeine to get through this, and anyway, wasn't it normal for someone to make the police a cuppa when they paid a visit? It wouldn't look odd, would it? She decided she didn't care, putting a cup beneath the spout and pressing a button for a latte.

"Not for me, thank you," Colin said, "but Jacob would probably like one. Two sugars."

She got on with it, weirded out that the officers weren't speaking now, just watching her make the coffee. Should she say something? It was better if she did that, wasn't it? "I can't believe I'm making drinks when something might have happened to my husband. He could have wandered out after he'd broken the window…"

"Why do you think *he'd* break a window?"

She took the cup over to Jacob who stood by the island. "Like I said earlier, suspected dementia. He panics sometimes, as if he's trapped in the house. He spends a lot of the time in the garden because he said the walls close in on him if he stays indoors for too long. He thinks they actually move." She went back to the coffee machine and selected the latte option for herself. She ran a hand through her hair, hoping she looked sufficiently puzzled and alarmed—and worried, she mustn't forget that. "What was it you had to tell me?"

Colin held an arm out towards the island. "Best if you sit. I'll bring your coffee over."

"What are *you* going to drink?" she asked.

"I'm a Pepsi man."

"There's some in the fridge there."

He seemed pleased by that and opened the door, taking a can out and placing it on the island, then collecting her coffee and bringing it over. He took two coasters from a stack in the middle beneath the vase of flowers she'd put there yesterday morning, which seemed days ago now. Jacob put his cup on a coaster, taking out an electronic notepad.

You can do this, you can do this, you can do this.

She pulled her cup towards her, coaster and all, and lifted the drink to her lips. Colin allowed her two swallows before he sat and placed a hand on her forearm. She put her cup down, knowing what was coming next. She'd need her hands free to cover her face while she faked hysterics. She looked at him, her lips trembling all by themselves, her eyes filling with tears.

Maybe this wouldn't be so difficult after all.

"I regret to have to inform you that your husband's body has possibly been found on the Cardigan Estate."

"What? His body? *Possibly*? What does that mean, you don't actually *know* if it's him?"

"I've received a photograph of him that was on file, and I'm ninety-five percent sure it is him, and there was a wallet found by the body with photographic identification in it and also a note, presumably written by him, but I prefer to say possibly until a DNA test has been done."

"Right. A note?"

"Yes. He confessed to upsetting someone, although we don't know who that is, and it also said he deserved what he got." Colin glanced at Jacob as if to let her know he couldn't talk as freely as he wanted to.

"You said body…" She shivered.

"Yes, I'm afraid he's deceased."

A second shiver went through her, so violent her body jerked. She wanted to laugh her head off, dance on his grave that didn't even exist yet. "I *told* Nathaniel something was wrong. I *said* Henry was going to wander off at some point, confused because of those stupid bloody sleeping tablets and whatever the hell's going on with his mental state. He shouldn't really have even had the pills, he must have got them online or something because I know damn well he hasn't been to the doctor. He wouldn't entertain it at all, not even for the dementia angle."

"He may have gone without your knowledge," Jacob said.

"I suppose."

"And Nathaniel is Henry's son, yes?" Jacob asked.

They must have done checks before they came here. God. "Yes. He's going to be devastated. He comes here most days to visit his dad."

"Why did Henry need sleeping tablets?" Colin asked. "I know that may sound like a stupid question, because sleeping tablets are to help people go to sleep, but what I mean is, were there any underlying reasons why he *couldn't* sleep?"

"He's retired, unofficially, but he doesn't share anything to do with the businesses with me, so the insomnia was probably work related. I asked Nathanial whether something was going on, but he said Henry kept things from him as well. Oh God, should I ring him?"

Colin glanced at his watch. "Let's just give you some time to digest this first. It's a very big shock. I also have to inform you that Henry was likely murdered."

"*What*?"

"This may sound like another silly question, but you *are* aware that Henry was a leader, yes?"

"Yes, of course I am, but he wasn't actually running the Estate. Nathaniel's been doing it for him. Both of them are really nice people, they don't go running around like some of the other leaders. They actually want to help the residents, to encourage them to be more of a community, so if you're going to ask if Henry had enemies, I can't think of anyone. He spent most of his time in the garden this summer, didn't go out much, just had his daily chats with Nathaniel, and sometimes his men come and visit. But there's Foxy, the gardener, too. I've been going shopping on my own these days, he's getting too old to walk around for such a long time. I go to the supermarket, do everything really."

"You say that he must have got the sleeping tablets online…"

"I assume so. I've never actually seen them arrive in the post, I just see him taking them out of a blister pack and swallowing them." Thank God she'd put his fingerprints all over the packets once he'd zonked out last night—and she'd flushed the plastic casings down the toilet inside a wedge of tissue. "We have CCTV, so we could have a look through it and I can let you know which deliveries are mine and which aren't."

She'd steered the conversation this way on purpose. She had to get it onto the visit from the man who'd delivered the note regarding Paddy's murder. She took her main phone out of her pocket, accessing the app for the cameras and selecting the one over the front door, going into the section that recorded when somebody activated the motion sensor.

"Oh my bloody God," she shrieked. "Look, there's someone in a hood putting something in the letterbox early in the morning yesterday."

Colin leaned over to have a look. "Maybe Henry had the pills delivered by dealers. Is that people you think he would have had access to?"

She stared at him in disbelief. "I have no idea. I don't know *what* to believe anymore."

"You said he doesn't wake until nine usually," Colin went on. "Did you not see anything on the floor by the front door when you got up and came downstairs? A padded envelope, anything like that?"

"No. I don't recall even looking at the door when I came down, then I stayed in the kitchen until about eleven."

Colin nodded, seemingly pleased with what she'd said. "Good, good."

Chapter Eighteen

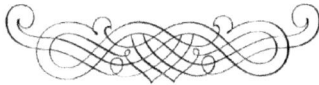

Eight o'clock in the morning, and already the air above the tarmac shimmered from the heat. Nathaniel and Bunny walked from his flat, down Wright Road and around the corner, heading for the café, a betting shop on one side, a laundrette on the other. Bunny had on a light-pink velvet tracksuit, looking so young that it could seem like he was cradle-snatching. A woman walked towards them with her dog, giving Nathaniel a filthy look as though she thought exactly that. Her animal panted, and no wonder, the day was going to be sweltering in about an hour.

The cafe's pink-and-white-striped awning had been pulled out above metal tables, the front ones catching the sunlight and glinting. Salt and pepper pots, along with menus and cutlery, stood in little wooden boxes beside vases with plastic roses in them. The outside gave a completely different idea as to who the owner was—cute and fluffy she was not; she swore like a docker. Nathaniel's first impression of the place years ago had been to expect fancy lattes, iced coffees with posh syrups, and pastries that cost a fortune. How wrong he'd been. The menu was more like a greasy spoon, except the food wasn't actually greasy.

They stepped inside, and it was an immediate relief from the steadily building heat on the street. The air-conditioning was on full pelt, not a sweaty face in sight. Art deco paintings covered the walls, and the scent of coffee, bacon, and eggs had drawn him here many a time. They sat at a table by the window, so he could easily be seen by anyone passing by. He nodded to a few customers who glanced his way.

Hattie, the owner, came flying over in her jean dungarees and pink vest top, notepad in hand. "What can I get you?"

"Two lattes and two fry-ups, the works, please," Nathaniel said.

"Everything okay?" She glanced at Bunny and then back to him, her question not directed at him in the way Bunny would likely think. Instead, Hattie was checking whether her ex was going to be causing her any more problems, as in had Nathaniel got him sorted out yet.

He smiled at her. "Everything's absolutely fine, thanks."

"Brilliant. Your food and drinks won't be long."

Nathaniel stared out of the window, hoping he got to eat at least half of his breakfast before he got the phone call. Bunny browsed her phone, her overnight bag on the chair beside her. The silence between them wasn't awkward, she often pretended to be his girlfriend if he needed to meet people who could potentially benefit the Estate, no questions asked.

The coffees arrived first, then the breakfasts five minutes later. Nathaniel had one sausage, a few beans, and half a slice of toast left when his mobile rang, Karen's name on the screen.

Bunny glanced at it and widened her eyes. "You'd better get that if she's ringing you. There might be something up with your dad."

It unsettled him that her mind had gone straight to that, but he told himself it was a logical thing for someone to think when your stepmum gave you a bell and your dad was old.

"Yeah, she only ever rings when there's a problem." He pressed the green circle icon to take the call. "Karen? Everything okay?"

"I'm so sorry, but can you come over? The police are here. It's your dad...he must have got out last night, there's a broken window, and...and..."

"What? A broken window?"

Bunny's eyes went even wider.

A scuffling sound filled his ear, then Karen whimpered.

"Hello, sir, I'm Detective Sergeant Colin Broadly. Would it be possible if you could come to your father's home as soon as possible, please?"

Nathan relaxed now he'd heard the copper's name. Whether the twins had managed to get their fella in on this, or it was a happy coincidence, he didn't care. "Of course. I'll be there right away." He ended the call and looked at Bunny. "I said I'd drive you home, but that was before. I've got to go to my dad's. You were right, something's happened, so do you mind if I take you to his house with me and arrange a taxi for you from there?"

"That's fine, whatever you need. You've paid me until midday, so if you need me to hang around…"

"I don't know yet. We have to go."

He left forty quid on the table for Hattie, waving at her to let her know it was there, then rushed out, Bunny trotting to keep up behind him.

"I'll run back and get my motor," he said. "Sit on the wall and wait."

He ran to his flat, going to the car park out the back and getting in his Audi. He collected Bunny and, much as he wanted to break the speed limit, he kept just below it, making it to the house seven minutes after Karen's call. He swerved the car onto the driveway, narrowly missing a vehicle he didn't recognise, the gravel shooting up in the air and dropping back down loudly. He got out and rushed to the front door, ringing the bell several times. By the time the door opened, Bunny stood beside him.

A young police officer in uniform gave Nathaniel a look of sympathy.

"Is my dad all right?" Nathaniel walked in and brushed past him, saying over his shoulder, "We've been worrying about dementia lately, but he won't go to the doctor." He headed to the kitchen, checking Bunny followed.

The poor cow was earning her money this morning.

Karen sat at the island, her eyes red-rimmed and her cheeks pink from tears. He wanted to go straight to her and draw her to him, but they'd agreed it was best she acted like a stepmother and that she'd been devoted to his father.

"Oh God, what's happened?" he asked.

Karen didn't flinch at the sight of Bunny coming into the kitchen, she'd known this was going to happen. She glanced at an older copper in a rumpled suit sitting beside her who stood and came towards him, holding his hand out. Nathaniel shook it, hoping he looked bewildered.

"DS Broadly, but call me Colin. It's best you take a seat." He switched his attention to Bunny. "And you are?"

"Belinda Forbes, but call me Bunny," she said, mimicking him. She stared around at everybody, her gaze finally landing on the young copper as he joined them. She sat at the island, her hands in her lap. "I'm Nathaniel's girlfriend, which is what I think you wanted to know."

"Right." Colin smiled then swerved his gaze towards Nathaniel.

Keep it together, you've got this.

Bunny had gone into another room with the PC to give her account of where Nathan had been since she'd met up with him yesterday. Nathaniel had furnished Colin with a rundown of his movements, Karen crying quietly in the background, getting up to look out of the window into the garden.

"Do you know of anyone who'd want to hurt your father?" Colin asked.

"No one. We don't run our Estate like some of the others do. We don't like any violence."

What he'd failed to say was that was only on the surface, but then if Colin was in with the twins the man would know exactly what really went on underneath, but this was an exercise in pretending, going through the motions.

"We're interested as to why your father was left on the Cardigan Estate—me and Jacob will be going to speak to George and Greg Wilkes today, and officers from divisions around London will be visiting the other leaders."

"Are you saying the twins did this?"

"Absolutely not, but it could have been made to look like it was them."

Colin was cut off by Bunny and Jacob coming back in, and then the doorbell rang, giving the moment an air of madness about it with too much going on at once. Nathaniel couldn't stand being in the same room as Karen without being able to comfort her, so he got up to answer it, finding Foxy on the doorstep.

This is becoming a fucking circus.

"Um, two seconds, wait just there," Nathaniel said and returned to the kitchen to go and get Colin. "I'm not sure whether to let him in or not, he usually pops in for a coffee before he starts work, but the gardener's here."

"He's not going to be able to stay, I'm afraid. Forensic officers will be here shortly." Colin left the room to go and deal with it, the floorboard in the hallway creaking.

Nathaniel turned to Bunny. "Do you want me to get you an Uber, love?"

"As long as you don't feel you need me here."

"No, I'll be fine; I'll ring you if I get upset. Let me just go and get your bag out of my car."

Nathaniel scooted past Colin and Foxy in the doorway, taking a moment by himself to collect the bag and inhale and exhale deeply. Things were going to plan, and so long as they could get through the next few days where the police followed leads and came to dead ends, then they could get Henry Greaves buried and off their backs for good. His father's friends were going to be spoken to, but as all gangsters knew, you made out everything was hunky-dory when it came to coppers poking their noses in. It was just a case of holding their breaths and waiting for the storm to pass.

Nathaniel had a leader meeting soon that he had to attend, where he'd admit to what had really gone on so the others didn't put their foot in it when the police came calling, but he'd have to wait for Colin and Jacob to leave first. He'd suggest getting Karen set up in a hotel while forensics were in the house, and he needed to find out what was going on about the sleeping pill angle. The twins had already sent a message to all leaders to ensure they kept out of the way and avoided the police until after the meeting. Nathaniel had been instructed to send a message once he was on his way to the warehouse so everyone could also head there.

Colin came back and sat next to Karen.

"I've just been thinking," Nathaniel said. "Someone must have broken in last night and taken my father away while he slept, because he's on some heavy-duty tablets where he doesn't wake up at all overnight. There's CCTV back and front, so you'll need access to that."

"Karen's already shown me. Someone came yesterday morning and put something through the letterbox, so we can assume that was a delivery of sleeping tablets, and as for the back, Foxy accidentally nudged the camera in the garden with the end of a rake while he was sweeping up after mowing. This done a couple of weeks ago, so there's no footage of whoever got in through the back."

That was a fucking decent coincidence.

Cheers, Foxy.

Nathaniel adopted the appropriate expression. "I hope you're not suggesting he did it on purpose or that he's got something to do with this, making sure the camera was out of the way long before anything happened."

"He's agreed to go down to the station and give a statement regarding his alibi. He didn't strike me as someone who'd known about this prior to coming here today. The poor man's shocked; he said he was good friends with your father and they spent a lot of time together while he did the gardening. Did you know who your father was getting the sleeping tablets from?"

"No. Who delivered them, a courier?"

"They had a hood on, and their face wasn't visible, unfortunately. They must have parked on the road, as they arrived on foot, and we couldn't see if there was a car because of the high hedge out the front. The pills will be taken away for analysis so we can find out exactly what they were, seeing as they've come from an unknown source. Karen said they're not in branded boxes, just plain white ones, and I suspect he got them on the black market somehow. I assume he has a laptop that can be looked at? And a phone? His browsing history might reveal if he purchased them from somewhere."

"No laptop, and he had an old phone, it wasn't a smart one. If they were bought online then someone else would have had to do it for him."

Karen sniffed. "I feel sick at the thought of him approaching someone else about it instead of just going to the doctor—or even telling me. I'd have suggested he tried those Kalms rather than whatever it is he was taking."

The doorbell rang again, and Colin went off to answer it.

"That'll probably be SOCO," Jacob said.

"I'll get you booked into a hotel, Karen." Nathaniel went over and patted her back. "I'd rather you weren't here to see people rooting through the house. You've got enough to deal with emotionally as it is." He looked at Jacob. "Will she be allowed to pack a bag?"

The copper nodded, smiling sadly at Karen. "I'll have to go with you, I'm afraid, to monitor what you're taking. Protocol."

Karen stared at the island. "I'm living in a nightmare. This can't be happening."

Nathaniel turned away to look outside. Not being able to laugh at her dramatic acting was excruciating.

Chapter Nineteen

Dear Diary,
    Most people would have walked away when Riley explained it all, but I stayed right where I was in that Merc, my mind churning over the possibilities. Two years of being married to some old man,

and then I'll be rich. As his widow, I'll get left a shitload of money.

No more living in a council house. I can spend my days shopping instead of working. I'll own soft cashmere jumpers, designer clothing, shoes, bags. I'll holiday in a posh villa abroad, sunbathing all day. It'll be built into the side of a cliff, windows reflecting the sunlight. I'll come home with a tan. I'll look gorgeous, and it would be a big fuck you to my mum who said I'll never be pretty enough to get anywhere in life.

You don't have to be pretty, Mother, just determined to get what you want. And I'm more determined than most. I'll have a whole room dedicated to clothes, a walk-in wardrobe full of everything I've ever wanted. I'll hang it up, colour coordinated, the rails like some rich bitch's personal rainbow. One of the walls will be full of shoes. God, I can see it all now. Riley said if I play my cards right, my future husband will hand over a credit card and leave me to it.

I'm going to have a big jewellery case full of diamonds, rubies, emeralds, sapphires, every single shade of gem there is, another rainbow I can look at to remind me I finally got the pot of gold. And a car, I want a fast one, sporty, a convertible. Riley said the husband-to-be won't want me to be seen going around in some battered-up secondhand motor. He's got a reputation to maintain.

I've got a phone Riley gave me. We can only message on it for now, and after the conversations we must delete them all. I can't let the husband know I have it. The only time me and Riley will ever talk on that phone is when it's done, the husband's dead. There will be meetings, though, where I'll pick up the prescription-grade sleeping tablets from Riley and give him updates on how things are going.

But first I have to snag the old man's attention.

Wish me luck!
Love from,
Karen Marie Livingstone

It turned out easier than Karen had thought. The last time she'd seen Riley, he'd told her to wait, he'd sort things, and all week she'd been waiting, only to receive a file from the agency and see the old bloke she had to marry was a new customer. He'd turned up in a posh car, and it was outside the pub now. In the toasty warmth coming from an open fire, brass horseshoes hanging from the mantel, she stared through the frost-rimed window at it, taking a deep breath and then stepping into the mardy weather to approach the vehicle, checking the number plate matched the one she'd been given.

L3ADR 1. Bentley. Blue.

She took another deep breath, walking around to the passenger side, seeing as though it was obvious he wasn't getting out to open the door for her. Riley had said for her to expect a lack of manners, but the prize at the end of it would be worth it. For the first time, she worried that what she was walking into wasn't something she'd be able to cope with for two years. On paper it looked simple: get a man to marry her, live with him while drugging him every night so she could avoid having sex with him too often, then someone would kill him, his Estate passing on. The reason for two years was so it didn't look obvious she was part of the plot. She'd have to pretend to grieve, although to be honest, she had a job and a half ahead of her to convince people in his life that she wasn't after him for his money, because what young woman would want such an older man? As in decades older?

She opened the car door and bent over to look inside. He matched the picture in the file, although he was a lot older than the one Riley had shown her.

She was going to have to have sex with a wrinkly.

She smiled to hide her shudder. "Henry Greaves?"

He smiled back. "That's me." His voice sounded scorched from years of smoking. "Hop in."

She wasn't about to hop for anyone, instead climbing inside seductively, making sure the slit of her dress parted to reveal an acre of thigh. The scent of the leather interior wafted—so this was what luxury smelled like, was it? So much headier than Riley's Merc. She closed the door then put on her seat belt, hoping the dress she'd chosen didn't scream 'desperate cow' but 'woman you're going to want to marry'.

He pulled away from the kerb, sending a quick glance her way and then concentrating on the road. She pretended not to notice and forced herself to go into work mode.

"How was your day?" she asked.

"Boring. You were recommended to me, so you'd better not disappoint."

Bloody hell, talk about abrupt and rude, but she found that a lot of men who had money were. The entitled bastards thought they could speak to her however they wanted because she was getting paid to put up with it.

"I haven't had any complaints so far," she said.

"Ah, but is that because you haven't offered extra services after hours? That's where many women fall down, underperforming in the sack."

Two years with this man. Really? "I've never done after hours before."

He slid his attention across to her again, his eyebrows raised. "What, a pretty girl like you hasn't been propositioned?"

"Oh, I have, I just haven't liked anyone enough to take them up on their offer."

He smiled smugly at the view through the windscreen. "I'm sure I can change that."

His arrogance pissed her off. Who the fuck did he think he was? Ah, that was right, the leader, Henry Greaves, the man she was going to enjoy earning money to trick, the man whose money she was going to spend like it was water, a bonus of fifty thousand *pounds and then whatever she inherited off him at the end of the line.*

She couldn't think of this not happening. She had to see it through.

"We're not going out for food," he said. "I'd rather we go straight to my place. My son arranged for a chef to come in and cook. He hired a waitress as well, so it'll seem like we're out anyway."

Her stomach fluttered with nerves. She'd expected to have sex with him tonight, but in a hotel, not his home, and she'd also expected several dates before she even saw the inside of his private space. Then again, Riley said Henry liked to brag, so it shouldn't be surprising that he'd want to show off his wares straight off the bat, a cock flaunting his plumage.

The car slid through the wet streets, the tyres creating slapping sounds with every rotation, and Henry had to put the windscreen wipers on as rain tapped on the glass, its beat getting steadily faster. The urban landscape changed to rural, and soon he turned into a driveway with a massive house at the end. Just the size alone hinted at how wealthy he was. It was so far removed from where she lived that she considered pinching herself to check whether she was really here. To think that she might actually live here—not might, she would live here—was a dream come true.

He parked close to the oak front door, getting out and heading towards it, leaving her sitting there, shaking her head once again at his discourteous behaviour. She followed him inside to a wide hallway, proper polished marble on the floor, the real deal, its muted grey and black veins subtle enough not to clash with a chair to the left and an occasional table to the right. The crystal chandelier likely cost more than she could imagine spending on something like that, the teardrops reflecting the light, sending it dancing on the white walls.

To her right, an elegant living room, and she longed to sit on the squishy cushions of the sofa and relax while she tried to seduce him, but he walked off towards the rear of the house. She poked her head into the lounge, admiring the mantelpiece that was taller than her, such a grand thing that it overpowered everything else. She eyed the ornaments on the top, betting they were antiques.

She stopped being nosy and found him in a kitchen, and it was exactly as she'd expected, all mod cons, a large island. The cupboards clearly weren't from IKEA, most likely made by a carpenter, probably a one-of-a-kind design. She glanced at a wine fridge that was as high and wide as the doorway and stocked with about seventy bottles.

This was the start of her mission for Riley, but also for herself. She was going to fulfil the promise she'd made years ago, that no matter what it took, even murder, she was going to be rich.

It wasn't going to be plain sailing, she knew that, and suspected there would be times she'd question her sanity in agreeing to do this, but every step of the way she had to remind herself that there was money to be had.

What better incentive was there?

Chapter Twenty

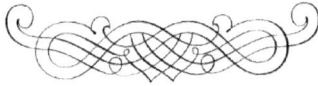

Nathaniel had been to leader meetings before with his father, so this wasn't new to him, but it did feel different without the old man there. Better. Fucking liberating. It was nice to know he didn't have to report back, Henry telling him he hadn't done this or that correctly, hadn't said the right thing. It was a weight off his mind knowing he didn't have to answer to anyone except the people in front of him, and even then that was only to a certain degree.

The Greaves Estate was his now.

All of the other leaders bar one had gathered in the twins' warehouse. The absent man was on holiday and would be sent the minutes so he was aware of what he had to say to the police when he returned home.

Nathaniel sat at the head of the table, as this meeting was essentially about him and his father, and poor Karen who would have been killed if Henry had his way. Everyone else sat and waited for him to start, hot drinks in front of them, a couple of trays of bacon sandwiches brought at a café on the way here. It was too early to have a curry, something the twins usually provided when it was their turn to host.

"So what's going on?" Jet Proust asked. "Apart from the fact Henry's dead and we've been told not to say anything to the police until after this meeting. Who the fuck says I *want* to talk to the police? I don't want them in my business."

She sat beside her right-hand woman who went everywhere with her. The pair of them unnerved Nathaniel, the way they seemed to read each other's minds, but he wasn't about to tell them that, it would swell Jet's head, the blingy cow.

"It's a case of *having* to speak to them this time," George said, nice and calm. "We all need to stick together and support Nathaniel on this one."

"Hurry up then," Jet said, staring at Nathaniel.

He wanted to tell her to fuck off but instead let everyone know about the deal in Italy. "So I turned to George and Greg and asked for help. While they weren't happy about stepping on another leader's toes because he wanted to bump his wife off, there were a couple of other things I told them that sealed the deal. Henry Greaves also killed his first wife, my mother, his excuse that he was bored of her, the same one he used to me with Karen. But there was something else, something I hadn't told anyone until the twins." He looked around. "I was abused as a child by Henry's friends, while he sat and watched— they're now dead and dealt with, by the way."

Murmurs went round, full of disgust, and a few people shook their heads.

How…weird that he didn't feel sickened at himself anymore. Or ashamed. Especially announcing it to a load of leaders.

He straightened his shoulders. "So he was dispatched. The police are going with the angle he was murdered because of some turf war or other, but you lot need to disabuse them of that notion—you were nothing to do with it. I'll plant the seed that it was a drug deal gone wrong; he was taking sleeping pills, so it'll be plausible."

He glanced at George who seemed okay with what he'd said so far.

Nathaniel continued. "So the gist of it is, according to the twins' copper who was at my dad's today, you're going to be spoken to and asked whether you had a beef with Henry. Obviously the answer's no. It'll eventually come to a dead end, case closed."

"Has anyone got anything else they'd like to discuss while we're here?" George asked.

Jonty Worth spoke up. "My daughter missing. Cara. She never came home and isn't answering her phone. I'm fucking fuming because she's been hanging round with that cunt from your Estate." He pointed at Nathaniel. "Oscar Carter. Know him?"

Nathaniel frowned to cover the fact that his heart hammered and his arsehole spasmed. *Christ, what…?* "Was she with him last night?"

"I don't know."

"Because I ordered for him to be killed then, and he was, so it's unlikely she was with him, otherwise my man would have said Oscar had company. His brother's also 'disappeared', if you catch my drift."

"Why?"

"My dad decided it'd be fun to watch them rape Karen. She told me about it, and I offered to get her away, but she was too scared to leave him." Utter bollocks. They'd hatched a plan to kill Henry instead. "She put on a front that everything was fine between them, so I had no idea of what went on during their marriage until she blurted the truth. So I got the Carters sorted. That was another reason why I wanted Henry killed, because of the way he treated Karen. But as for your daughter…. I'll have a word with my man, see if he's seen her. If he did then I'll let you know where."

The chatter moved on to other things, scrotes to be aware of who were straddling the borders between Estates and doing dodgy shit on either side, and shared deals that needed discussing, but Nathaniel's mind wasn't on any of it. He had to speak to Best, *now*, couldn't sit here gossiping with this lot when something so monumental might have happened regarding Jonty's daughter.

Or could he be worrying about nothing?

He stood, everyone's attention swivelling to him. "I'm going to go and see my man now. I can't settle if I know a girl's missing. How old is she?"

"Seventeen." Jonty took his phone out and scrolled, pointing to her picture.

"Can you send that to me so I can show my bloke?"

Nathaniel left the warehouse, getting in his car and using his burner to send a message to Best that they needed to meet, his hands shaking. He drove to the empty street behind the Galway Arms, getting out to cross the road and go into the yard. He inspected the tarmac for blood, but as usual, Best had done a bang-up job with the cleaning. He went inside the pub, leaving the door unlocked, and sat on a stool in front of the bar to wait.

An overwhelming swish of anxiety swept through him, the impending meeting worrying him more than he'd like to admit. A voice in the back of his mind whispered about implications regarding Oscar's murder, suspicions that Nathaniel hoped weren't true. His pulse sped up, his heart skipping a beat.

What if that girl was here last night?

Worry simmered until it reached a boil so violent he got up and paced.

Surely Best would have told him if he'd deviated from the plan, wouldn't he?

Chapter Twenty-One

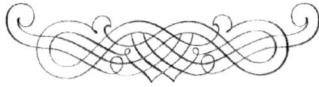

Best hoped this meeting was only a face-to-face chat regarding Oscar Carter. If it wasn't… Sod it. He may as well admit to the cock-up anyway, *before* Nathaniel had the chance to pull him up on it. He could say he hadn't wanted to send any messages, even though it was a burner-to-burner communication, considering the implications — and ramifications — of the dead girl being the daughter of a leader.

Yeah, that sounded right. He reckoned he'd get away with that line of chat.

It seemed all he'd done since the murders was sigh in between racking his brain to see if things could have been any different, but the outcome always ended up the way it had been in real life — there was no way he could have let the second person get away, no matter who she was. It was an absolute shitshow, if he were honest, one hell of a mess that he might not be able to get himself out of. Nathaniel had him bang to rights on so many things, could get him nicked just like that, the evidence against him so high Best couldn't deny it — or he could, but no policeman on the planet would believe him. But that was only one angle Nathaniel could take. There was death, and then that posed two different possibilities. Nathaniel himself could kill him, or he'd hand Best over to the girl's father to do the job.

I'm going to have to explain how it went down and hope things turn out okay.

He turned the corner, and the closer he got to the pub, the more hesitant his steps became. The day had morphed into another boiler, sweat trickling down the middle of his back and into his arse crack. Not a fucking cloud in sight, the sky a perfect blue. He wished this was just a casual stroll, his choice to be en route to the Galway, but if Nathaniel clicked his fingers, then Best had to come running.

Fuck running in this heat, though.

Thoughts of the impending encounter were loaded down with his unspoken fears—he'd never say it out loud, and who could he tell anyway, but Nathaniel had such a hold on him that sometimes Best wished he had the guts to end it all. Yes, his factory was doing well, the money was coming in and he wanted for nothing, especially with the extra cash payments Nathaniel gave him for the use of the smelter, but what he had to put himself through emotionally to get that… Sometimes he couldn't believe who he'd become. Never would he have thought he'd kill someone. Now there was a whole list of someones, and he'd become Nathaniel's bitch.

He stepped out into the road to give a mother with a buggy enough room on the pavement, the cobblestones hard beneath his boots. He rehearsed the upcoming conversation in his mind, although from experience he knew damn well it wouldn't work out the way he imagined it would. When you had another person in the picture, it tended to change things; they had their own shit to say.

With each passing moment, the shake of his hands became more prominent, and he honest to God reckoned he ought to run away. He turned a corner again, glancing across at the properties on the other side of the street to see if anyone watched him. He couldn't tell from a couple of houses because they had thick nets at the windows, and anyway, the cover story for him keep meeting Nathaniel here was they were discussing how to do the pub up—but that wouldn't fly if, for any reason, word got out that a couple of murders had been committed in the yard. The police would be all over it like a shot, and even though he'd cleaned the blood, they were bound to find some he'd missed.

He walked to the back of the pub and stood beneath the uncomfortable heat that the sun blasted out, his heart beating far too fast. He stared at the road where his van had been parked; Nathaniel's car was there. Heat created a haze off the road like some weird wavering mirage, a smudge in the atmosphere that didn't look right.

His palms sweated, and he rubbed them on the arse of his jeans. Every second he wasted here was only going to ramp up his anxiety, crunch his lungs way too tight.

Nathaniel's previous warnings set up home in Best's mind from the night their alliance had first been cemented: *Don't even think about backing out of this. You've got no choice but to do what I say, Best. We're partners now.*

He pushed open the gate, left unlocked. It creaked, which it hadn't done last night. He closed it, pausing for a moment, then walked across the yard. The back door was also unlocked. He stepped inside, his stomach lurching. The stale air smacked him in the face, the whiff of ancient ale spilled so long ago, and cigarettes, the scent of the smoke living in the walls. He poked his head into the office, and a laser of sunlight entered through the broken window. Nathaniel was bound to have noticed the splintered glass from outside on his way in.

That's probably the least of my worries.

Best's heart drummed hard, a cruel hand of fear twisting his stomach. He continued along the corridor, coming out behind the bar. Nathaniel sat to the left, and their eyes met in the semi-darkness.

"Tell me about last night," Nathaniel said. "All of it."

"Exactly what I intend to do. There's no way I was sending what went down in a message."

Nathaniel winced. "Go on…"

Best joined him at the table and explained what had gone on, stopping for a breath at the point he'd spotted the second person. The memory of it flashed into his mind—if only things had been different, if only she hadn't been there… He continued the tale until he'd shot both people and gone outside. He felt sick, knowing what came next. "I pulled the bandana down, and it was a fucking *girl*. I recognised her an' all."

"Right…"

"Cara Worth. You know—"

"Yep, I know." Nathaniel stood and walked to and fro, his face in shadow, all the curtains closed.

The place was so gloomy it gave Best the creeps.

"Thanks for not lying to me—and for being considerate regarding not sending a message with her name in it." Nathaniel stopped and raked a hand through his hair. "I assume they both went in the smelter."

"Yes. Why wouldn't I have done that?"

"I had to check. I've been to a leader meeting. Cara being missing was brought up."

"Shit."

"The dad's aware she hung around with Oscar. I told him he was killed last night and that I'd ask whether anyone else was with him."

It felt like the bottom of Best's stomach had fallen out. "He doesn't know *I* killed Oscar, does he?"

"No, I just said I'd have a word with my surveillance man."

"About…"

"Whether you saw Cara with Oscar at any point in the past week."

"No, he was usually with his brother, never women."

"Hmm, I wonder if she lied to her old man about who she's been with."

"I don't know, but why would she even do that? Oscar was a right wanker, someone no man would want his daughter hanging around with, so unless she was seeing someone who was *worse*… Do you see what I mean? Better to say she was with Oscar than someone who could really do her some damage."

Nathaniel nodded. "It's kind of by the by because she's dead."

"No it isn't. You go back and say she wasn't seen with Oscar, then her dad's got to wonder who she *was* with. He'll poke around, eventually find out, and they'll probably get a grilling as to where she's gone. He's not going to want to involve the police in her being missing because of what he does for a living and who he is, so he'll investigate it himself behind the scenes. He'll just have to face the fact she's all but an adult and went off to do her own thing. She cut contact with the family."

"He's not going to be able to keep it from the police. She's seventeen."

"Why not? She's over sixteen so can legally leave home. I doubt very much her movements are going to be tracked to here. If you think about it, they came on foot, her face was covered, and it was dark, so unless they got themselves seen on the way, then I'd say we're safe."

He recalled how he'd only seen one person crossing the street towards the pub, and that person had looked over their shoulder as if waiting for someone to follow. Or, as Best had assumed, worried that they were *being* followed. It made sense now that it was the former, or maybe the girl had been waiting out the back all along, before Oscar had arrived.

Should he tell Nathaniel that or just leave it? "I only saw one person cross the road. After everything had happened, I cleaned the yard, and I can do it again now it's light, get some strong bleach. I'd have to go and pick up my van, though. I walked here."

"You do that. I've got to go. There's stuff to do. My dad's body was found this morning."

"Shit, sorry to hear that."

"I'm not. Wait for ten minutes before you leave to get your van. Lock up after yourself."

Nathaniel walked out, leaving Best to ponder what the bloke had said—that he wasn't sorry his father was dead. Which now meant Nathaniel was the official leader of the Greaves Estate, even more reason for Best to toe the line.

He leaned against the wall in the corridor, staring at the door to outside, wishing he could walk out and never come back, but there was a yard to bleach.

He left the pub and locked the door, standing in the yard to give it a proper good inspection. He couldn't see any blood on the ground so moved to the crumbling wall—that was where any problem would be, the rough surface, the nooks and crannies and holes created by bits breaking off. And speaking of the bits, he'd have to sweep them all up, and while he was at it he'd take the old beer kegs to the factory tonight and melt them. Take everything in the yard, actually.

Out on the path, he locked the gate, choosing to walk down this street instead of the residential one at the front. He didn't want to be seen, obviously. More than that, he didn't feel like being sociable, and if anyone he knew stopped him for a chat, he was likely to internally blow his stack. He couldn't be seen as out of sorts in any way. Not when he'd killed two people last night.

Chapter Twenty-Two

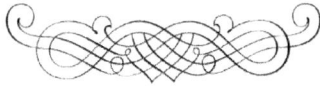

Colin had to be careful during this visit with the twins. He had Jacob with him and needed to constantly remind himself that he couldn't behave like he usually would while in their company. Now he fully understand how Janine had felt when she'd been skewing investigations for the twins and he'd been with her, asking questions, putting spanners in the works and generally getting on her wick. He couldn't fault Jacob, though, the kid was good at his job and didn't act overbearing.

It was strange to go back to being a copper with George and Greg, but it was something he was going to have to do in order to get their names out of the investigation other than that they'd been spoken to and eliminated. Anyway, what was he on about, he was doing *them* the favour, not the other way around. Colin had already driven to Jackpot Palace, sending Jacob in to ask if the twins were around. At that point, he'd messaged to let them know they'd have to be in The Angel within ten minutes so that he and Jacob would just happen to bump into them.

"So what interactions have you had with the twins previously?" Colin turned at a corner and quickly glanced at the PC, then back at the road.

Jacob stared ahead out of the windscreen; if he'd looked left out of the passenger window, it might have indicated he was trying to hide his expression from Colin, but the man seemed at ease and with nothing to hide. Colin didn't think he himself had behaved oddly today, nothing for Jacob to report back on, but it was never far from his mind to worry that he'd slipped up somewhere and hadn't realised it.

"There was an argument in the street a few weeks ago," Jacob said, "and they were there trying to calm a couple of residents down. I turned up in a response vehicle, and they were nothing but polite to me. I know people say they're arseholes, or they can be, but they were nice enough to everyone involved in the spat, basically calmed everything down for me."

"Yeah, but we mustn't forget they're leaders and bloody good actors the way they behave in front of the police as though butter wouldn't melt. I want you to watch their faces when I ask questions, see if you can pick up on any lies."

"Right."

Colin swerved into the driveway next to the pub. The twins' BMW was there as well as Debbie's Mini. Colin smiled to himself. Maybe they'd roped her in as their alibi, or it could just be a coincidence and she was actually visiting her own pub for once. She was barely there now, too busy enjoying her life with Moon.

They got out of the vehicle, and Colin led the way into the pub, his stomach full of nerves. He glanced around casually as though he didn't expect the twins to be there, then gave Jacob a nudge when he saw them sitting at a table with Debbie who had a few pieces of paper on a clipboard on her lap. Colin approached them, Jacob just behind.

George looked up. "Ooh, the Old Bill. Everything all right? Did you get confused and think this was the station?"

"Is there somewhere we can have a little word?" Colin asked.

"What about?"

"Your alibi for last night and the early hours of the morning."

"Err, early hours we'd have been in bed, like normal people. As for last night, we were here well after closing time with Debbie and Lisa."

Even though he knew who she was, Colin asked for Jacob's benefit, "Who's Lisa?"

"That woman over there who runs the place for Debbie."

"How long did you stay here for?"

Greg seemed bored with the conversation. George glanced at Debbie.

"It had to be about two-ish," she said, "because I remember looking at the clock and thinking I needed my bed. We sat here for a little bit more, maybe ten minutes, then… Actually, hang on…" She took her phone out and scrolled WhatsApp, showing Colin her screen. "As you can see, that's the time I told my husband I was just on my way home." She moved to another chat. "And this is where I let Lisa know what time I'd be arriving here for our meeting."

"Do you have another chat where you asked George and Greg to join you?"

"No, because they were already in here when I turned up, and the meeting initially had nothing to do with them. I asked for their opinion on revamping this place. It's tired, the paint needs livening up. They've got two pubs that they've just done up, so I picked their brains." She repositioned the clipboard so Colin could see the papers she fanned through. "I wrote everything down that we need to do, and today we're adding any bits and bobs we've thought about since last night. They say you need to sleep on something before you make a final decision."

Colin looked at George. "Did you do anything else after you left here?"

"We went straight home."

"Which route?"

George told him, and Colin hid a smile at the fact that there were no cameras. And even if there were, they'd have ensured they were switched off by Bennett or John, the CCTV operators they had on their payroll.

"Can anyone verify the time you got home?" Colin asked.

"Me," Greg said. "I was with him."

"Thanks very much for your time, gentlemen." Colin walked towards the double doors, sensing Jacob not far behind. Once out on the street, he waited for the PC to join him. "What did you think?"

"That the cost of replacing the flooring is a bloody fortune. Did you see that estimate on one of her bits of paper?"

"No. And I didn't mean about the revamp."

"I know, but I couldn't get past the prices for a second. And no, I don't think they had anything to do with Greaves. I found it odd they didn't ask why they needed an alibi, though. Most people would, wouldn't they?"

"That's true, but maybe because they haven't done anything they didn't feel the need to know the ins and outs. They likely get asked about their alibis a lot so it's become normal to them. Boring.

Anything else you think I need to be made aware of?"

"Yes." Jacob stared across the road at a man standing in an alley, then he returned his attention to Colin. "I also find it weird that considering they're leaders and a body was found on their Estate this morning—and there's no way they wouldn't know about it—they didn't ask you any questions, they were sitting in a pub chatting renovations when I'd have thought they'd be out there trying to find out who'd killed Greaves. Not that they'd know *who* it was if they hadn't had anything to do with it because no press release has gone out yet—"

"—that we know of."

"Yeah, that we know of."

"So we're in agreement that they have nothing to do with it."

"Agreed."

Colin headed towards the car.

"Where to now?" Jacob asked.

"We nip back to the Greaves' house to see how SOCO are getting along. They might have found something that sends the investigation in a different direction."

They got in the car and on the journey talked about Jacob's life—his girlfriend was pregnant, and they fancied moving out of London to somewhere quieter to bring their child up, plus he felt a rural position was better suited to a father as he constantly worried he'd be injured on the job in London. The subject inevitably changed to the cost of living and how much cheaper it was elsewhere.

They arrived at the house twenty minutes later. This time they put on protective clothing, despite the fact they'd been there earlier and had definitely left fingerprints, fibres, and hairs. As they'd switched location several times since they were last here, Colin didn't want them to drop any fibres they'd brought with them. Anything here from Jackpot Palace when it shouldn't be would really fuck things up.

The first port of call was the broken window. It had definitely been smashed from the outside; the pattern of glass on the floor indoors was a big indication of that.

Hua Chen, one of the forensic team, must be smiling at them as her eyes crinkled over her mask. "Have you come for a little update?"

"Yes, please," Colin said.

"Window broken from outside, the remaining glass removed and placed against the outside of the house—the purpose of that, I have no idea, because I don't think anyone entered through the window. I've been out and noted that the lock for the patio door has a new scrape on the outside of the barrel where the usual key possibly wasn't used and something else was instead."

"Like a pick?" Jacob asked.

Hua nodded. "Yes."

"So why bother smashing the window when they got in via the door?"

Hua shrugged. "Maybe there were two of them and one did the window just in case the pick didn't work."

"Plausible," Colin said. "Covering all bases, getting things done quicker if they were both working on the entry points at the same time. Anything else?"

"Nothing of note in the back garden that will give us an indication of who this was—Wilson's out there now going over the grass again, but it's not looking likely that he'll find anything."

"Because of the glass," Colin indicated to the floor, "have you been able to follow the trail to see where they went when they came in?"

"So far, no glass has been found elsewhere, so I suggest they entered through the doors, skirted round the table, and left the room without going anywhere near any shards or fragments. I'm just about to swab the inside of the window frame, but to be honest, I'm not hopeful that anything will be collected. They are *so* likely to have worn gloves—or I would if I were them. It's common sense."

"Yet we know a lot of criminals don't have any." Colin sighed as though disappointed no leads were forthcoming in this room, when deep down he was relieved. "Thanks anyway."

She nodded and turned back to her work.

They walked the rest of the house, Jacob pausing at the doorway to one of the bedrooms.

"Did you believe Karen when she said she sleeps in this room because Henry snores, yet still uses earplugs as well?" Colin asked, wanting to get an idea of what was going on in Jacob's head.

"Yes. My mum and dad do the same thing, and she wears earplugs because his snores come through the wall."

"Yet Karen's still got all of her possessions in the bedroom she used to share with Henry."

"Again, that's the same as my mum and dad. They're only sleeping apart; my mum reckons if she took all her stuff out of the bedroom it'd feel like they'd split up or something."

"I suppose. A psychological thing." Colin stepped backwards to look into the marital bedroom. Definitely only one side had been slept on, the quilt turned back neatly instead of thrown off in a hurry. "Whoever it was wasn't in a rush to remove him from the house." He pointed to the bed once Jacob had come over.

"Maybe they knew he took sleeping tablets."

"What do you think happened regarding Karen? Did they pop their head in on her, saw she was asleep, and then moved on to get her husband out of bed, or did one of them stand here and keep watch in case she woke up and came to investigate?"

"It could have all been done by just one person, which is completely doable. Karen isn't exactly Marvel superhero material, she'd be easily overcome by someone giving her a punch or two in the head, so I doubt very much they were bothered about her being here other than she might wake up and phone the police."

"Or she knew about it beforehand and they didn't have to worry about her waking up because she'd said she'd stay in bed." Another test on Jacob's perspective.

"I didn't get the feeling she was in on this at all. The poor cow was in bits."

"I feel the same, I'm just playing devil's advocate. We have to look at every single angle. What about the son? Did you think his alibi was just a bit too…too rehearsed?"

"No, because I read the statement you took from him, and it's very similar to Bunny's. They both remembered things the same way, in the same order, and I know that in some cases that looks like they've conjured up an alibi together, and they've both gone over and over it so they're on the same page, but there was so much going on for them from when they first met up that one of them would be bound to forget something if they'd made it up. Anyway, there will be CCTV, plus a record of him using the Uber from outside the Bell, not to mention the taxi they got in outside Intoxication. They'll be on street CCTV and everything."

"So we've established it's neither of those two, but out of curiosity, what did you make of her? Bunny, I mean."

"I don't see them being in a lasting relationship, she just wants a bit of fun at the moment, but she was nice enough, didn't come across as anyone to be suspicious about."

"So do you think it's like Nigel said, a gangland feud?"

"Probably. Henry was disembowelled; hardly your average stab wound, is it."

"Then there's the note that was left behind."

"Yep. Even without it, I'd say he pissed someone off and they came for him."

Satisfied they were on the same wavelength, Colin jerked his head for Jacob to follow him downstairs. "I'll message Nigel and see what he wants us to do next."

It would likely be everyone gathering at the station to share information. Colin glanced at his watch and smiled.

It looked like he might get some lunch after all.

He nudged Jacob. "Fancy a blueberry muffin?"

Chapter Twenty-Three

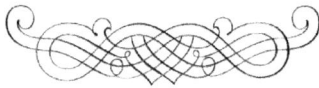

Dear Diary,
How to say you hate it somewhere without saying you hate it? How do you pretend you love every aspect of your life when you abhor it? How do you admit that you may well have bitten off more than you can chew?

Every bullshit thing Henry's ever done has been documented here, so I'm going to have to burn the diaries that feature anything to do with my part in this fucking insane quest for money. And it does feel insane. Utterly mad. There can't be any evidence that could be used against me, to say that I killed him, or arranged for him to be killed. Actually, just before he gets murdered, I'll burn every single diary I've ever written, because a lot of them involve my dream to be rich, which could also send pointing fingers my way.

I've had sex, I've cooked, I've cleaned, I've taken abuse, verbal and physical, and I've been humiliated on my wedding day by Henry taunting me beneath his breath, all endured by me in silence. Whenever Riley comes here, I wish I could tell him what's going on, but it has to wait until I can find some time to get out of the house and meet him for a secret chat—and to collect the pills—because to try and do it in this prison of a house when we could so easily be seen, heard, and caught, would send Henry wandering down a path he shouldn't go down.

There is no way my husband can know we're in cahoots together.

And things have taken an even more hideous turn. I am NOT okay. I've just been raped by two of Henry's friends while he sat and watched. I didn't sign up for this level of horror. I realise I'm swindling a man out of his money, having already convinced him to leave me the house and half of his money, but the price I'm paying is soul-destroying.

I don't know if I can do this anymore.

Love from,

Karen Marie Greaves

Henry had gone out, Karen suspected to that pub, the one down by the river where everything stank of mould and salty water. A poker game, apparently, him going off with his two friends as though he hadn't just paid them to violate her.

And why was an old man hanging out with young men anyway?

Their marriage had been a weird one, where he'd told her right from the beginning that he didn't want a traditional wife in the sense that they'd actually care for each other, just that she was there for show and for a hole that he could plug when the fancy took him. It'd suited her—until he'd opened the front door to let those men in earlier on.

With a promised storm lurking, she left the house shortly after him, taking her little convertible and parking down a residential street, a huge, abandoned park opposite the houses, the land bought by developers months ago. It didn't even look like a park anymore. The grass was so overgrown it would reach her knees, or so she judged by seeing it through the wrought-iron fence. The swings and roundabouts and the slide had long been taken away, the area left for nature to run roughshod over. And it was so creepy and still over there, but it was somewhere she'd suggested meeting where they wouldn't be seen together. With Henry out and about, maybe not even at the pub, she couldn't risk the usual hookup at a hotel. Those nights were reserved for when she'd drugged Henry with extra sleeping pills.

She thought about Riley. She was starting to get feelings, and so was he—or had he just said that the night she'd told him she didn't think she could keep going with this fucking horrible nightmare anymore? Had he promised they could be together afterwards to keep her trying to eat the dangled carrot?

She crossed the road and opened the creaking gate, shoving it to push down some of the grass to give her enough space to slip inside. Riley had said he was coming in from the opposite end so their cars weren't seen in the same place. She waded through the grass, and the bloody stuff turned into whips, curling around her ankles and trying to trip her over. She walked past a patch of tarmac, weeds pushing up through the cracks where maybe a slide had been bolted down, then she waited by the big tree like he'd told her.

A bench squatted under it, the branches so low and heavy with leaves that she took the chance to have a sit down, satisfied she'd be shielded enough. She'd walked into a monochrome world once she'd entered the park so couldn't see what colour the paint was that peeled off the bench slats, but she imagined it was once vibrant red or blue. The air had a damp feel to it, and she cursed herself for not bringing an umbrella.

It was hard to imagine that people lived a couple of hundred metres away. It was so quiet here it felt like she was in the middle of nowhere, although now she came to listen hard enough, she caught the faint hum of distant traffic, maybe a front door slamming shut.

Then a gust of wind came out of nowhere and swept through the branches. She shivered, the memory of what had happened in the bedroom earlier coming to the forefront of her mind. She shoved it away—it was going to be bad enough recalling it in a minute with Riley, so why torment herself twice?

Something rustled in the foliage behind her—either in the grass or some of the unruly bushes bordering the fence on the inside—and she jumped up, facing whatever it was, ready to run if she had to. She peered at a dark shape that came crashing out of the hedge. A badger waddled along and then disappeared in the shadows farther along. The incident unsettled her more than she cared to admit, and now she imagined someone was staring at her, and they were standing in the bushes and that's why the badger had run, because it had been disturbed.

"Stop it," she muttered.

Another set of shuffling had her spinning round. A silhouette came towards her, and she recognised it as Riley, thank God. She sank back onto the bench, gripping her knees to give her something to steady her racing heart and mind.

He sat beside her. "What's happened? Why the urgency?"

It all came spilling out, her recent ordeal and the crappiness of her life in general.

"I didn't have a shower in case I needed to go to the police," she said. "I wanted to see what you had to say first."

"No police. They'll be dealt with, all three of them, but give me time. Those two friends of his have a habit of bragging about what they've done, and if they've gone to play poker like you said, you can bet they're going to be laughing about it. If they end up dead or disappeared come tomorrow—or even inside a year— it's going to be obvious you told someone. In this game you have to pick your battles, and this is one we'll ignore for now."

"What?"

He promised everything would be all right, that he'd fix it, and then he was walking away, all tight angles and sharp strides, his hands in his pockets and his head down. As always, after she'd met up with him, she got the wobbles. She rose and hurried over the grass, every footstep creating swishing noises. She sensed she was being watched again, from that bush behind the bench, as though Henry knew she'd leave the house tonight and his announcement that he was going to play cards was a ruse to make her think she was safe. Could he have followed her here? Of course.

Was he the type to keep it to himself until a later date? Yes.

She was going to have to act like nothing had happened, regardless. It was the pattern they'd formed, the life they'd created together, the dominant husband and the submissive wife.

She still had so much more to endure until he was murdered.

Unless she could get it done sooner.

She reached the gate, the wind picking up and slapping into her face, streaming through her hair. She rushed across the road towards her car, and the first fat raindrops fell at the same time the sky grumbled with thunder. One droplet landed on her cheek, cold, and dripped down, and soon tears joined it, although they were hot and stung her eyes. She got in the car, and the downpour began in earnest, slapping onto the bonnet, drumming hard and loud. She sat and watched the wet sheets going down the windscreen, the view ahead blurred. She started the engine and switched the wipers on, doing up her seat belt and waiting for the heater to kick in. The nearby streetlamp glowed with a fuzzy orange halo, and as she warmed up, it slammed into her how reluctant she was to go home, even though Henry wouldn't be there.

That house wasn't what she'd expected it to be. It was a badge of wealth, yes, but she had no friends to show it off to. She spent most of her days flicking a feather duster around and trying to listen to any conversations Henry was having with visitors, although he inevitably told her to piss off, in front of them, which was totally embarrassing. Even more so was him telling people she gave decent blow jobs and that was all she was good for these days.

Next time she should bite his cock off.

The rain came down harder, the street indecipherable, or maybe that was her tears turning her vision hazy. She blinked and set off, looking forward to a shower, and burning the sheets, burning the underwear she'd had on when those men had—

She wasn't going to think about it, just wait to be told that those men were dead. She'd put things into motion to make sure Henry died sooner rather than later. And that meant speaking to Nathaniel about the rape. If Riley wasn't prepared to get a move on, she had a feeling Henry's son would after he found out about this.

Considering they'd been having an affair for the past six months without Riley knowing.

A girl had to hedge her bets.

Chapter Twenty-Four

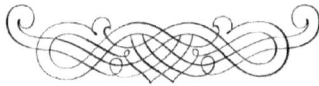

George's second-best friend, Ralph, panted in his ear, the dog's head poking between the front seats of their little van. Ralph was having a break from doing the protection money rounds with Martin—George usually left them to it, but he'd missed the doggy today, mainly because one of the other leaders had mentioned getting a puppy. Ralph would have to be crated at home later, though, as they were having a meal with Colin at the back of the Taj at five, where they could discuss business in private.

It was a bold move for the copper to have spoken to them out in the open at The Angel, with customers clearly earwigging, but to have got up to talk elsewhere, it would have made them look like they were hiding something. Had it been Colin on his own, George wouldn't give a shit, but he'd had that young copper with him, the one who'd turned up to deal with the street fight a couple of weeks ago. Nice kid.

"Can you stop the car for a minute?" George asked Greg.

Greg did as he was told, and George got out, leaving the passenger door open; Ralph wouldn't wait for him to go round the back to let him out. Instead, as George had predicted, the animal jumped between the seats and followed him onto a patch of grass. After a quick sniff, Ralph cocked his leg against nothing and did a wee, then sat with a paw up.

"I'm not playing ball here, it's a *verge*, not a bloody park," George said. "Now get back in the motor."

Ralph jumped in and sat on George's seat.

"Get in the back."

Ralph just sat there, so George took the harness off the hook behind the seat and clipped the dog in. He shut the door and went to the back, getting inside and settling on a wheel arch.

"That dog rules you," Greg said.

"Nope, I just couldn't be arsed to argue with him."

"You don't argue with a dog, George, you tell it what to do."

"Whatever."

The journey continued, George doing his best to seek out misbehavers on the streets from his position this far away from the windscreen. A couple of hours of rounding up any small-time villains would pass the afternoon nicely, not to mention taking his mind off something that had been troubling him ever since the leaders' meeting.

Cara Worth. He'd got Mason, their private detective, to have a nose into the girl. He hadn't found much online except an Instagram account, but when he'd put on a disguise and gone to the Worth Estate to ask questions about her—fucking brave of him, considering Jonty might have got wind—a few flashes of cash and he'd got some interesting information.

Cara wasn't a sweet seventeen-year-old but a little cow intent on causing trouble everywhere she went. Her brother, Ben, came out more favourably, an amenable person compared to his sibling who thought nothing of slapping people around and demanding free drugs, drinks in pubs, and meals in restaurants, basically saying, "Do you know who I am?"

Maybe someone had got pissed off about that and decided to teach her a lesson. Or had she got caught up in being with her friends and had forgotten to tell her father she wouldn't be going home last night? Or was there something more sinister going on? George wanted to get hold of Nathaniel and ask if his surveillance men had spotted anything regarding her, but he might be with police officers, ones other than Colin, and he didn't want the man to have to try and explain who was on the phone. It would have to wait until later, once they'd spoken to Colin and knew whether Nathaniel would be asked to give any more statements. But surely if Cara had been spotted then a message would have gone out from Jonty, saying panic stations over.

Something didn't sit right.

Chapter Twenty-Five

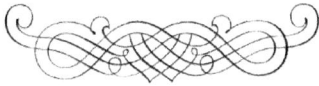

Because of the Cara issue, Nathaniel had spent quite some time going through his options. He had to think about himself here, how he would be perceived, and not allow guilt to poke at him. His father may have been one of the biggest arseholes on the planet, but he'd been right when he'd said that if it was a case of lying, going to prison, or being killed, then lying won hands down.

And he was going to have to lie.

He'd made the decision to get rid of Best. That way, the man and any association with him would be gone. Except he couldn't do it himself, not while the police were in his life, and he didn't want any of his other men to do it either. The less people in the know the better. He'd be forfeiting the use of the smelter; with Best gone, his brother would, without a doubt, shut down the one Nathaniel and Best had been using. Tom had been saying for a while to Best that it was a waste of money because it wasn't used.

So he bloody thought.

Nathan would have to find another means of disposing of bodies, but it wasn't something he had to worry about at the moment, especially because he intended to play the good leader, the same as he had when he'd been helping out his father in running the Estate. People thought he was lazy, because he didn't go round scaring people half to death (publicly; in private was another matter). There *had* been torture and murder, and the eventual deaths of various irritating residents, but no one had attributed them to him.

He preferred to play behind the scenes, just like he was about to do now.

He picked up his phone, toying with which number to send a message to. The twins or Jonty. Or maybe he should start a group chat so he was being open with them all at the same time.

He thought about what he was going to say and then typed.

Chapter Twenty-Six

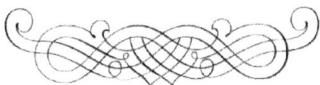

At eleven minutes past midnight, while he sat in his house drinking a cuppa, Best had a horrible feeling. It sat deep in his gut, in that cavernous space where he knew he shouldn't ignore it. It was the same space he'd had the feeling that his mother was going to die, despite her assuring him the tumour wasn't aggressive and the hospital had said radiotherapy would be enough to shrink it.

It hadn't been enough.

It hadn't shrunk.

She'd died.

Was this another premonition about death? His own or someone he knew? Likely his own, but Nathaniel hadn't seemed overly bothered about him killing Cara, so maybe Best was just being paranoid there. Nathaniel hadn't stomped about and thrown a punch or two to vent his anger regarding Best making the decision to kill both people in the yard. It was as if Cara being there was nothing but an unfortunate mishap and it was inevitable she'd be killed as well as Oscar. *You never leave witnesses*, that was one of Nathaniel's rules, so Best had only been doing as he was told anyway.

He'd absolutely done as he was told. If the second person had been anyone other than a leader's child, then there wouldn't even be a debate about it. But that feeling, it was too strong, not something he was prepared to ignore. So he was going to go and stay at his hideaway flat, the one he'd rented in Tom's name, just in case he needed somewhere to go in a hurry. He'd been there a few times, and it felt like a holiday, a nice break from real life. He'd hole up until the gut feeling went away—and preferably until the initial search for Cara by the Worth lot had died down.

But would a father really stop searching for his kid? If it were Best, he'd keep going and going until his dying day, but he'd heard Jonty was more for his son, so maybe things *would* die down eventually.

He packed a few of his belongings to take with him, but not much as he had clothes and disguises already there. He never went to the shops round that way without a fake beard on, and he always changed his accent to Welsh. The neighbours thought he used the flat as a little getaway, nosy bastards that they were when he'd gone there for the first time, grilling him stupid. A quick stop on the way at the overnight Sainsbury's, and he'd get some basic shopping; he wasn't sure if he'd used all the UHT milk he usually kept there. Takeaways would do for dinners.

He'd leave the van behind the factory after he'd burned any clothing and footwear he'd used when murdering for Nathaniel. He'd tell Tom he needed a break, life was getting on top of him again, the excuse he'd used when he'd first started working for Nathaniel, which was when he'd handed the reins over to Tom regarding the business. He kept his car at the factory whenever he wasn't using the van, so he'd go to the flat in it and park it out of the way in the garage. Besides, it was what he always drove when he went to the flat. The neighbours would clock a different vehicle quicker than he could blink.

He gathered his things together and put the black bag of murder clothes in the back and his small holdall on the passenger seat in the van, which could really do with a bleach job inside, something he'd do before he left for the hideaway. Maybe he ought to dump the water flagon and hose in the smelter, too, in case there was any blood on them; mainly the hose where it would have dragged on the road and through the yard.

Or just burn the whole van.

That wasn't a bad idea, and it would be a symbol, cutting off this life and starting another. He might just stay in the flat and grow a real beard, pretend he was the Welsh businessman forever.

It appealed. He wanted a new life more than he'd realised.

He drove off, heading for a petrol station so he could buy a can and fill it.

The night's darkness and past-midnight shadows cloaked the factory, the only light coming from the two faint bulbs in the lamps either side of the back door, only there to give enough illumination for whoever needed to slide a key in the lock. This place had been his whole life at one time, something he'd built up by himself, employing his brother and teaching him the ropes.

The large smelter chimneys poked into a pitch-black gulf of sky, the tops barely visible when he craned his neck back to look. He walked round and used the side door, disarming the alarm—maybe he ought to change the PIN on that and send the new one to Tom. Nathaniel wouldn't be able to switch the alarm noise off without it, and it'd be a message to him that he couldn't dump bodies there anymore. But what about if Nathaniel realised Best wasn't coming back and he turned his nasty attention on Tom?

I'll leave it.

Inside, the stillness always bothered him, how damn quiet it was, the air prickling with silence, always raising the hairs on the back of his neck. He shut the door, carrying the black bag, the flagon, and the hose. He'd emptied the flagon to make it easier to carry.

His footsteps clonked on the wooden flooring, and he paused at a chill going down his spine; either something was wrong here, in this factory, his gut feeling from earlier something to do with this place, or he was imagining it because the empty building had always given him the willies. It was as if people watched him from the corners, so many eyes. The sense of being observed followed him all the way to the smelter room, only ceasing when he shut the door and switched on the light.

He loaded the things into the smelter then sat on the floor to give himself time to think before he raced off to the flat. All those people he'd helped to disappear without a trace entered his head, their families desperate for news of them, and he knew where they were, or where they'd ended up, just a few feet away from him. In the other world, the one he'd lived in before he'd met Nathaniel, he'd never have believed anyone who'd told him he'd willingly put a dead person in his smelter, but life had a habit of sending you down pathways you didn't have the directions to, you just blundered on until you reached a clearly signposted crossroads at last.

The only directions he had this time were dictated by common sense. He had to get away, at least until any uproar about Cara had died down. He couldn't imagine Nathaniel telling Jonty she'd been killed by one of his men—he risked being blamed for her death just as much as Best; if Nathaniel hadn't ordered for Oscar to die, then Cara would still be alive, that's how Jonty would see it, but that wasn't the case at all, was it. Neither of them had known Oscar was the man behind writing the note about the twenty grand until he'd appeared in the fucking yard.

Best switched his mind to his mother, then. If she were alive, she'd be so upset he'd gone down this route. She'd brought her sons up to be good boys, and she'd succeeded until Best had grasped the hand of greed and run with it. She'd have said he could have got out of working for Nathaniel if he'd tried hard enough, and maybe she'd have been right.

It felt like she was watching him from wherever she'd gone after she'd died, shaking her head a little, and guilt swarmed in on him from all sides. He even swore he heard the beep of the machines in the hospital, that incessant swish of whatever had been keeping her lungs functioning. He remembered the feel of the chair beside the bed, how he could never get comfortable in it. He'd held her hand in his; hers had seemed too small, like a child's, and he'd cursed himself for not seeing how much she'd shrunk over the years, how much age had stolen her robustness and given her fragile bones instead. He'd been too busy building up the factory to see what was right in front of his face.

It was no use thinking about her, it only served to make him feel bad. Already a knot of grief had filled his throat, his chest burning with the need for a sob to come out, but crying had never helped him, had never solved anything either, just left him exhausted, with a headache and puffy eyes and the massive need to go and get drunk.

When she'd died, some of the weight had come off his shoulders because he hadn't had to worry about her anymore, but the majority had still been there because of Tom. Being older than him, Best had always felt responsible; he'd promised their mother he'd always look after him, especially because Nan and Grandad weren't around either—another thing Best blamed himself for, but he wasn't going there tonight. Anyway, Tom wasn't this little lost soul who needed saving like Mum had always seen him as, he was strong and resourceful and ran the factory much better than Best ever had.

The dream of a new life had started to take root. If he told Tom he was going travelling, his brother would only ask if he had enough money to do it. Maybe, because of the gut feeling, it was better to tell Tom exactly that so he didn't think the worst had happened if Best didn't reappear ever again.

Don't talk daft, he'd at least think something had happened to you if you didn't come home.

The idea of not seeing Tom again upset Best enough that tears stung his eyes. These thoughts he was having threatened to suffocate him—fuck this shit, he needed to leave.

Back in the car park, he put gloves on and set about soaking the interior of the van with petrol. He left the driver's window open a tiny crack, enough for him to post in a burning match, and the oxygen would help feed the fire. The flame hit the seat, and he ran. The whoosh of the petrol going up was loud behind him, giving him a jolt, and he stumbled to get the keys out of his pocket, the ones for the car. He got in and drove away, using the quiet route where he was less likely to be seen.

His grip on the steering wheel tightened when he thought about the ramifications of what he'd done. He doubted anyone would even see the van on fire, the factory was out of the way, and the building shielded the car park from any roads and houses in the distance, but come tomorrow, the workers would see the burned-out shell and gossip would start.

Sometimes he could scream at how everything just seemed so hard. All he wanted to do was get the fuck out of here, go and curl in a ball and hide, but there was still shit to do first.

He pulled over into a lay-by to send a message to Tom.

SHANE: JUST IGNORE THE STATE OF MY VAN AT THE FACTORY. I ACCIDENTALLY SET IT ON FIRE; I HAD A CAN OF PETROL BECAUSE I WASN'T SURE IF THE CAR HAD ANY IN IT SINCE THE LAST TIME I USED IT. I

SPILLED SOME AND WAS SMOKING AT THE SAME TIME. I DROPPED THE FAG. FUCKING STUPID OF ME, I KNOW. ANYWAY, I'LL SEND SOMEONE TO TAKE IT OFF THE PROPERTY.

TOM: BLOODY HELL! I WORRY ABOUT YOU SOMETIMES. IF YOU HAD A BRAIN…

SHANE: LOL. SORRY AGAIN. ALSO, I'M GOING AWAY, NEED TO GET MY HEAD SCREWED ON STRAIGHTER. MY MENTAL HEALTH HASN'T BEEN TOO GOOD LATELY, BUT DON'T WORRY, IT'S NOTHING PEACE AND QUIET WON'T CURE. SEE YOU WHEN I GET BACK.

TOM: YOU KNOW WHERE I AM IF YOU NEED ME.

SHANE: YEP.

He looked up at headlights reflected in the rearview mirror, blinding, enough that he had to squint. Why was another car coming into the lay-by? Wasn't that odd, considering the time of night?

He set off again, a worm of unease wriggling—that gut feeling had intensified.

The car didn't follow, and he released a breath of relief. He was being paranoid, that was all, jittery because of the Cara thing.

A couple of hundred metres down the road, he checked the rearview again. Someone was behind. His heart leaped — *it's just another driver, nothing to worry about...* And he would have thought that was true if he hadn't had such a dreadful feeling for ages now. It was more than just a gut feeling, he felt completely sick and out of sorts. Dread grew, so he put his foot down, going an extra five miles an hour.

The car behind did the same.

Oh, fucking hell.

Maybe it was a woman on her own, and because it was a pretty deserted road and dark, she didn't like the idea of driving out here by herself. Somehow, his theory didn't hold water. He had the horrible sense that he was being tailed.

He went faster again, another five miles an hour, and the car kept up with him. He was convinced something serious was up now, so there was no way he could lead them to the secret flat. He was a good four or five miles from anyone he knew, and going from memory, he wouldn't find an open shop or petrol station for another three or four miles. Trust him to have taken the back roads that were more like the ones in the countryside. He was unnerved by the isolation, wishing he hadn't chosen this route. And to think at the start of this journey that his only issue was to avoid cameras, but he had to avoid death instead now as the car walloped into the back of his on the right-hand side.

The night pressed in on him; he was in serious trouble here if he couldn't get away. His headlights stabbed into the darkness, revealing the road ahead, but he needed more so put them on high beam. That was better, but it was just his luck that no other vehicles were coming towards him, therefore, he couldn't frantically flash at them to let them know he needed help.

He checked the mirror again. The silver radiator grille of the car behind was tinted red from Best's taillights as he swerved around a bend, then he was shunted off course and towards the middle of the road; the car careened into him again in a deliberate smack of aggression. The sound of the tyres going over the cat's eyes was so loud. The relentless crashes into his vehicle happened again and again, his car shuddering from the impact, adrenaline surging through him to the point he felt sick. To take his mind off the fact that someone clearly wanted him dead, he concentrated on keeping between the white lines on the road, his grip on the steering wheel sore on his palms, chafing. His arm muscles ached where he tried to maintain a straight line, but the car behind hit him again.

He fishtailed but managed to keep the bloody thing on four wheels. It scooted round with a screech until it faced the opposite way, and he sped off, past the other car, catching a glimpse of who drove it.

Jonty Worth.

Oh fuck.

Chapter Twenty-Seven

Nathaniel hadn't expected to stand here with the twins and Jonty, Best sitting on a metal chair, his calves trapped against the front legs, his wrists held together behind the chair back by the same special clips at his ankles. This wasn't how he'd envisioned things going, but he had to concede that he couldn't call the shots in this, not when it wasn't his daughter, when it wasn't his decision to decide Best's fate. On the one hand, Nathaniel would rather he wasn't here so he didn't have to watch a man die when he really didn't deserve it, but on the other, it was better that he was here so he could keep an eye on the proceedings, or more importantly, an ear on the things Best had to say.

I'm nervous in case he says shit I don't want him to say.

What if I can't get out of it?

They'd all gathered at Jonty's 'dungeon', as he called it, a space beneath one of his pubs that had been done up to look like some olden-day torture chamber, the walls sweating condensation, stinking of mould and mildew. An eerie silence had taken over as they all stared at Best who'd been crying and sported a tomato of a cheekbone and an egg of an eye. Dust motes flickered in the slice of light coming from a man-height version of an office desk lamp, its shade like a bonnet from *The Handmaid's Tale*.

The weight of Nathaniel's deception pressed in on him; he felt it in the way Best looked at him, his unspoken questions lingering between them: *It was you, wasn't it? You sent Jonty to follow me.* Of course it was, there was no way Nathaniel could continue with the façade of being a good and kind leader if he didn't pass information on to Cara's father—and in turn, it was an ideal way to get rid of Best without dirtying his own hands. He'd explained his relationship with Best and told them that Tom had no idea what the smelter was used for, so it was advisable that Jonty didn't pay him a visit. Best's brother knew fuck all so shouldn't be punished. Jonty had accepted this with good grace and surprising calm, considering he'd just received the news that his daughter was dead.

The man was probably boiling beneath the surface.

Jonty had sent a message to tell them all to meet, and he'd given directions to here, the Snake Pit, where people upstairs danced the night away with fashionable flavoured gins in hand with no idea a man sat on a metal chair waiting to be electrocuted. Electrodes had been clipped to the metal at Best's wrists and ankles, wires trailing away into the dark where the light didn't touch. It was as if he were under a spotlight, the star of a torturous show.

Nathaniel could only be glad it wasn't him, but as he knew in situations such as this, things could go wrong in the blink of an eye and it *could* be him sitting on that seat at some point. He hoped his relationship with Jonty was good enough that he'd be believed over Best, but if Nathaniel were honest, he'd never really had much to do with Jonty in order to build a good relationship.

He wished he'd listened to his father and forged friendships with the other leaders now. Yes, he'd kind of done that with the twins, but they didn't look too happy to have been ordered here, and who could blame them?

After Nathaniel had hit SEND on the message that had dropped Best right in the shit, he'd regretted his decision, his conscience barking that *he'd* been the one to bring Best into this dangerous world, Best hadn't chosen it. The man was an excellent killer, even if he hated doing it, and the smelter was most certainly handy, but Nathaniel's need to appear squeaky clean was more important than Best's loyalty and uses.

He couldn't allow this latest web of deceit to wrap around him, waiting for the spider to appear—and he had a feeling it would have if he hadn't taken action. So wasn't it better that the spider only got one of them? Although he had a feeling that now he'd drunk from the poisoned chalice, turning on his trusted man, everything may taste bitter from now on. Karma may well punish him.

Maybe in time, the feelings brought on by what he'd done would fade, he wouldn't feel so guilty for what amounted to a betrayal. Best had trusted him, and look what Nathaniel had done in return. But staying silent about that girl was worse than opening his mouth.

He shouldn't want to say sorry, but he did, and it wouldn't make him look weak if that's what he chose to do because he'd already told Jonty and the twins that he was a different kind of leader to them.

He was going to act on his thoughts. "I'm sorry."

Best stared at him with his decent eye and through the slit of the other. "You're sorry for telling the father of that poor girl that I killed her, basically on your orders. Is that right, or have I got something wrong here?"

Fuck. *Fuck*!

Nathaniel glanced to Jonty to see how that statement had landed—not very well. The bloke's expression wasn't a good one.

"Explain," Jonty said to Best.

"He told me to never leave witnesses, no matter *who* they were. I was supposed to end the man who'd come to collect the twenty grand, then I noticed someone else in the yard. I couldn't see who they were because they had a bandana over their face, and I couldn't kill one without the other. It was only after I'd done it that I could see who she was, and I swear to fucking God, I'm so bloody sorry."

Jonty eyed Nathaniel. "You should be sitting on a chair like that as well. If it hadn't been for your instructions, Best wouldn't have killed my daughter."

Nathaniel wasn't quite sure what to say. He'd likely put his foot in it either way. The twins weren't stepping forward with words to help him, so it was clear he was on his own.

How quickly people leave you to it when the shit hits the fan.

I should never have stepped into the limelight and apologised.

But then maybe Best would have blurted out his little story anyway.

Everyone's stares pushed against Nathaniel to the point he wanted to stumble back into the shadows so they couldn't see his face; it burned with shame, and if he was being totally honest, anger at himself, but mainly directed at Best for disregarding every threat Nathaniel had ever made to him and appealing to three other leaders in the hope they'd set him free. But to be fair to him, his life was on the line, and he'd do anything to save it.

Even dropping me in it.

Despite his blush, Nathaniel stayed within the cone of light, accepting the probes of their visual inspections, and it felt as though all of his faults were being exposed for them to pick apart. They were assessing him, probably working out which angle to go with, but ultimately, it would be Jonty's decision.

His pub, his rules.

His dead kid whose death needed avenging.

Nathaniel's irrational thoughts took over, spewing ridiculous scenarios. Any minute now, he could be stripped naked and paraded through the pub, everyone pointing at him and chanting

"Shame!" while they raised their gin glasses to Jonty as a nod of respect to his mourning. Jesus fucking wept, his mind was going haywire, thinking shit like that, but thank God he was Henry Greaves's son, brought up to hide his fears under a calm façade. None of these men would know that beneath it, he felt the same as any other human being in this kind of situation would—scared, vulnerable, and desperate to find a way out.

Just like Best.

Nathaniel was going to have to respond to what Jonty had said. The silence had stretched on for too long already. "That was something I had to tell him on behalf of my father. That isn't my rule. It isn't something I'll be asking for going forward because I don't intend for anyone on my Estate to be killed by me or my men if I can help it. I do understand where Best's coming from, but I was my father's proxy, so how can I be held accountable for basically following my leader's rules?"

That angle was something none of the other leaders could dispute.

"Very true," George said. "We'd expect any of our men to follow our rules, as would you,

Jonty, regardless of whether they agreed with them or not. If Best had left a witness, and Nathaniel had to go home to Henry and tell him there was someone out there who'd heard or seen Oscar being shot, there's no way Nathaniel would have got away with it without his father having a right go."

Jonty nodded. "But someone's got to pay for killing my Cara, so the pair of them can die." He looked from Best to Nathaniel. "Joint enterprise, both of you following your leader's orders, call it whatever the fuck you want, but if it wasn't for you two, my kid would still be alive."

"If your kid wasn't hanging around with Oscar Carter," Nathaniel blurted. "That's the real reason why she's dead. Or maybe it's you not keeping a better rein on her."

And just like that, he'd sealed his death warrant.

George wasn't going to step in and say a word, but he felt that with Cara being a bit of a cow, she'd probably have ended up getting herself killed anyway, it was just unfortunate that it had been Best who'd murdered her. Not that George was saying a young girl being gobby meant she deserved what she'd got, but basically, if Jonty didn't know how bad Cara had been, he was going to get justice for her anyway he knew how. And, George suspected, that even if he *did* know who his child really was, he'd want the same justice anyway.

George was conflicted. Nathaniel had been through a terrible thing as a child, and all he'd been doing was passing on his father's rules to Best, so did he deserve to die? Even if they were his own rules, Cara had been killed without anyone knowing who she was when the bullet had been fired. As for Best, he'd just been following orders. It was true, everyone wanted a killer to pay the price, but in this situation, George didn't feel that the two men should be held accountable.

It was the way of their world, but if he saw it through the eyes of a father, if he was Jonty, he'd want to kill the pair of them, too, even if it wasn't the right thing to do.

Catch 22.

Chapter Twenty-Eight

*D*ear Diary,
      Nathaniel is going to sort my
rapists tonight. He believed me
immediately, said it sounded like it was
something his father would do, but he
didn't elaborate on how he knew that. He
confessed he wants him dead, has done for

years, and then he told me something he'd been putting off for about a week.

Bear in mind that he's been running the Estate in his father's name for a while now. Henry's become lazy, he can no longer be bothered to enforce the rules, so he handed the reins over to his son, instead choosing to sit in the garden if it's nice, or the orangery if it isn't, and waste the hours away sitting on his recliner throne and drinking with visitors.

So Nathaniel told me Henry's arranged for me to go to Italy. The story is that I'll be running his new business out there, but the truth is I'll be dead, and Nathaniel will be the one to kill me. Except he said he won't, that Henry will be dead instead. I told him I was worried that with no body, there's no proof he's dead, therefore neither of us will get any inheritance. But he said the body will be left out in the open to be found, so there's a murder investigation, he just has to convince the right people to help him to do it.

But that's for another day. Today is the last one those two men will be breathing. Their names are Rob and Oscar Carter, brothers, and one of Nathaniel's men has been watching them for the past week. I don't know how it's going to happen, just that it is. It's probably for the best that way.

Love from,
Karen Marie Greaves

It was taking ages for Henry to settle down in the living room with his whisky. The stupid man paced a lot, as if he knew something was going on this evening. Karen tried to act normal, but knowing the Carters were going to be killed tonight, she couldn't help but have rattling nerves. She had to be so careful, though, because Henry was still sharp despite being old, and a couple of times he'd looked at her as if he was going to ask what was wrong, then shrugged as if he didn't care.

But he more than likely didn't, not now he was bored of her and planned to send her to her death in Italy. Maybe that was why Riley had chosen two years, because he knew Henry got bored quickly with whatever woman happened to be on his arm.

Karen had given Henry three sleeping tablets instead of two. It was better to be extra sure he wouldn't wake up when Nathaniel phoned her about the Carter murders. But two tablets were always enough, so she didn't need to worry at all, or maybe she secretly hoped it would end up as an overdose and she'd find him dead come the morning.

He got up to go to bed soon after he'd swallowed the last drop of his drink, slightly unsteady on his feet.

She smiled at the state of him. "Do you need some help?"

"I'm not that old yet," he snapped.

"Maybe we need to install a stair lift."

He shot her a seething glare, and she had to remind herself that he'd be dead soon and she wouldn't have to put up with him any longer.

She used the toilet in the main bathroom while he went into their bedroom. She waited five minutes so he didn't ask her to give him a blow job. She stood next to the bed now, staring down at him. He'd drifted off quickly—he hadn't even undressed and was under the cover in his clothes, nor had he switched off the lamp which cast his face in a strange yellow glow, as if he had jaundice. His breathing was slow and heavy, and *the spite he usually wore on his face in the form of a permanent frown was smoothed out. He almost looked like a nice person, someone's grandad. He was so vulnerable there, wouldn't be able to do a damn thing if she put a pillow over his face and pressed down hard, and even though the temptation was strong to do this by herself, she was going to leave his murder to professionals.*

She thought about the first time it had been clear that Nathaniel fancied her, when he'd stared at her for a little too long, and when she'd muttered to him in the kitchen that he'd have his eyes gouged out by his father if he wasn't careful where he pointed them. He'd said he didn't care, he'd look at her if he wanted to. She'd kissed him then, an impulse move, born because she trusted Riley but not completely and needed someone else in her camp.

Having three men on the go wasn't such a bad thing, was it?

She felt more on her guard with Nathaniel, though, despite him telling her she was becoming the love of his life. Did she really believe that? She kept waiting for him to turn on her, to say he'd been reeling her in to prove she was only with his father for his money. She wouldn't accept he wanted the same thing as her until Henry was actually dead.

If Riley or Nathaniel let her down, she'd never trust anyone again.

She leaned over to switch the lamp off, and the darkness nudged against her, pressing up tight until she shuddered and convinced herself someone stood there watching. She'd felt that a lot lately, dark gazes on her, but it was most likely guilt manifesting in the form of imaginary shadow people she couldn't see.

Henry snored. She had to leave this room. Get the fuck away from him. She'd stay in the spare bed again. She'd avoided this one ever since the Carter brothers had raped her. Henry had no idea where she slept — she always pushed down on her pillow in the middle to make a dent, scrunched the quilt on her side as though she'd been beneath it, which she did now.

She headed for the door and paused there, turning to face the window. Henry hadn't even shut the curtains. His snoring got louder, or maybe the room had got quieter, she couldn't be sure, but either way it was unsettling. It was more likely that she was on edge because of the countdown going on in her head; soon those brothers would be dead, and she'd be able to move on knowing they couldn't hurt someone else.

She walked out and closed the door behind her, pausing on the landing with her hands on the banister rail and, concentrating on her breathing, blocked out the sounds of the house as it settled for the night. She moved along the landing, going down the stairs quickly, heading for the light coming from the living room; it represented safety compared to upstairs. About to shut the curtains, she looked out the front into the summer night, the sky a weird purple-grey colour with a peach belly. For a moment she swore she saw someone standing to the side of the hedge that shielded the house from the road, but when she blinked they were gone.

She locked up, made a cup of tea, and settled down to try and watch the telly, but her mind kept drifting with her wondering which brother would die first and how *they'd die.*

Two hours later, she went to the spare room, putting the fan on and pointing it towards where she was going to be lying. She undressed and got in bed, folding the quilt back because of the oppressive heat. She switched the lamp off and closed her eyes, scaring herself with every creak or tap, every swoosh of a car going by, but not hearing the sound that she most wanted to—the one that signified a message from Nathaniel.

It came ten minutes later.

NATHANIEL: MISSION ABORTED.

The anger that flared inside her brought on a flood of tears.

KAREN: WHAT?

NATHANIEL: MY MAN COULDN'T GET A CLEAR SHOT. TRYING AGAIN TOMORROW.

KAREN: IS IT GOING TO BE THE SAME WITH PADDY? ARE YOU GOING TO LET YOUR MAN KEEP TELLING YOU 'MISSION ABORTED'? WE SHOULD DO PADDY OURSELVES SO THAT ACTUALLY GETS DONE. MEET ME TOMORROW AFTERNOON IN THE USUAL PLACE AND WE'LL DISCUSS IT.

Paddy Winchester was another pervert, and she planned to tell Nathaniel about every single one of them if she heard even a whisper that they were bad men. In fact, she'd like to kill that man herself. It would prove to Nathaniel she was up for doing anything for him.

In order for everything to go to plan, she had to make sure he believed every word she said.

Chapter Twenty-Nine

Electrocution was such a fascinating thing to watch when someone else was doing it. George stared at the way Nathaniel's arms and legs spasmed; his body jumped around, the chair going with him on some mad bunny hop, his screams the soundtrack of nightmares. Jonty had stripped him prior to forcing him to sit on the metal chair, Nathaniel fighting him all the way, swinging punches until George had gripped his wrists and held them behind him. It felt wrong somehow, to help subdue him when he didn't agree with his death, but this was Jonty's arena, his choice, and if this was up for debate at a leader meeting, there would be no question that someone had to die for killing Cara, so why not the man who'd given the order? There would most likely be a show of hands in Jonty's favour

Best sat on the floor out of the way, naked, with his hands tied behind his back. He'd asked to at least be allowed to tell them his side of the story before they killed him, swearing it wasn't as it seemed. George was inclined to believe him, but whether Jonty would remained to be seen.

This was a difficult one. What was going on here was none of the twins' business, technically, because it was happening on the Worth Estate and it involved two men who'd had a hand in killing a leader's daughter. But at the same time it *was* their business, because they'd been in allegiance with Nathaniel. George didn't want to piss off Jonty, but at the same time he felt that Best needed to be heard. The problem was, Jonty had a habit of reacting now and thinking about it later, much like George used to be, so it wasn't it better that he suggested Jonty take a breath between murders to see if the second one was absolutely necessary?

Even though Best had been the one to pull the trigger, would he have killed anyone had he not been working for Nathaniel? What kind of person had he been before they'd met? The answers to those questions would determine what should happen going forward. George would have to weigh and measure his words carefully, straining them through a sieve to weed out the ones that really didn't need to be uttered—the ones that would cause the most offence. He'd have to watch Jonty's face for the hint of a micro-expression that would tell him whether he'd offended the leader.

Jonty applied another burst of voltage to Nathaniel, and the stream of electricity flowing through his body did the job. Jonty switched it off, nodding to himself, seemingly satisfied that he'd killed the person who'd trained another man in how to work for him, which had resulted in the death of an innocent seventeen-year-old girl. Nathaniel went limp, his body slumping, and George glanced at Best to see how he was coping.

The man was understandably shitting himself.

Jonty stared at him. "Start talking, and you'd better make it convincing, because my blood's up now. All I can say is that it needs to be good, what you've got to say, because I'll think nothing of killing you, too."

"Tell him who you really are," George encouraged Best. "The person you were before Nathaniel came along and ruined you."

Best seemed to get what George was guiding him to say, and he gave a slight nod of thanks, then launched into the story about a man who'd had dreams to own a factory, give his mum the best life she could ever want, and make sure his brother had enough money to pay the bills. A good man who'd never imagined he'd raise a gun and shoot someone's daughter and God knew how many sons. A good man who'd never imagined his mother would die so young, leaving him without the rudder he'd held on to all of his life. He'd had to switch to Tom for reassurance and advice, despite his brother being younger than him, and Nathaniel had come into his life when Best had been vulnerable and in the midst of mourning his grandparents. He hadn't been thinking straight, he'd grabbed on to this new way of living to block out the grief, his feelings, and how much he missed his mother.

Nathaniel had manipulated him, used Best's emotions to his advantage.

And threats were terrible things, they forced you to do what you never would have considered once upon a time—George knew how that worked from his side of the fence. The amount of times he'd coerced someone to do what *he* wanted…he was no better than Nathaniel in that respect, so who was he to judge Shaun Best for the choices he'd made?

Jonty had offered to dispose of Nathaniel's body by his usual means, but George felt that making father and son look like they'd been killed by the same person would be the better way to go—a proper feud. Colin wouldn't be too happy about another corpse on the Cardigan Estate, but he was paid to do a job, and he'd just have to fucking well do it. He also wouldn't be happy about the different MO, strangulation versus electrocution, but George planned to gut Nathaniel and bleach him in the same way as Henry so at least there were some similarities, not to mention he was stark bollock naked and he'd be left on the grass.

What happened to Best was no longer in George's hands, and he'd refused to stick around to witness the outcome of Jonty's decision.

They'd park the taxi on the side of the road opposite an area that locals used as an oasis away from home, somewhere they could go and sunbathe and pretend they were anywhere but London. The air felt thick tonight, George's skin clammy beneath his clothes and a fresh forensic outfit. The smell of baked mud was back; the sun must have sucked up all the moisture from last night's storm. Humidity clung to his face, and he used the back of a glove to wipe the sweat off his skin.

Everything was so still, including Nathaniel on the grass, his arse facing upwards, the orange of a nearby streetlamp giving his skin an amber hue. Greg came over and handed George one of the heavy bleach bottles. He soaked the back of the body, the hair, and they turned him over to do the same on the front. He repeated his actions from before, cutting the belly like a pie and pulling out the intestines to drape them over the sides of the midsection.

Greg poured bleach over the knife and the blood on George's gloves, then they took the bottles and put them in black bags, placing both in another black bag that only Greg had touched as he wasn't contaminated with claret.

It was time to go home and dispose of the evidence.

Chapter Thirty

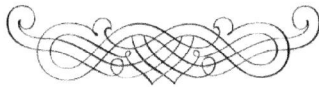

Karen sat in an elegant Edwardian chair positioned at an angle by the balcony doors in her hotel room. The view was of the thrumming city and its twinkling lights; everything was still so vibrant despite the hour, apart from the faint hum of the traffic ten stories below. A distant siren went off—the police never rested here—and it gave her a chill. Colin and Jacob had been nice to her today, they hadn't seen her as the woman who'd orchestrated her husband's death, and she hoped to God she was going to get away with her part in it.

But tomorrow she had to face the authorities again, to give a much more formal statement at the police station instead of Colin just taking notes. She hoped it would be him she spoke to but suspected it would probably be a PC, maybe one who wasn't as kind-hearted as Jacob had been, one with an air of indifference regarding her situation. Whoever it was, she'd maintain her weeping widow act and the confusion as to why someone would have disembowelled Henry, despite him writing a note. She'd seen a photo of it. Colin's boss had sent it to him, and she'd peered at his screen, nodding to say it was definitely Henry's writing.

She imagined him being forced to write it and smiled.

She and Nathanial had been over and over things until she almost believed the crap they'd come up with between them: Henry was a good man who wouldn't have had any enemies, he and Nathan wanting to run the estate in a kinder, more tolerant way compared to others, and she hoped to plant the seed tomorrow that perhaps the person who'd delivered the tablets had been the person to kill him.

The person who'd really supplied the pills was dead, disposed of once Karen and Riley knew he'd served his purpose.

She leaned her head back and closed her eyes to shut out the blinking reds of taillights, the whites of headlights, and the creams of lit-up windows. She imagined sitting on one of those hard chairs at a table in an interview room, an unimpressed officer opposite her, accusing her of being involved in her husband's murder. A tendril of panic rose up her chest to flutter at the base of her throat. It would be awful for the interviewer to stare at her, trying to break her, and even worse if Karen caved and blurted out what had really happened, but she couldn't, this had been planned for so long, and she was almost at the end.

Soon she'd walk onto the stage that was the Greaves Estate, no longer the wife of Henry or the too-young stepmother to Nathaniel. She'd be a different Karen Greaves to the one they all knew.

She opened her eyes and released a long, calming breath. A standard lamp with a soft, low-watt bulb stood behind her, its light reminding her of how long she'd been sitting here; she'd been reading for the past couple of hours, unable to sleep. Nathaniel had set her set up in an expensive place, and she had yet to use the phone by the bed to contact reception to come and collect the trolley that had been used to bring up her dinner earlier. It was all silver dome over a fine china plate, crystal glasses for water and wine, gleaming silver cutlery, and a rabbit made out of napkins. Despite the upheaval, she'd been surprisingly hungry and had eaten a chicken dish with a creamy sauce and the best mashed potatoes she'd ever tasted. The chocolate dessert had also been high-quality.

She'd leave the dinner trolley until the morning. They could take it when they delivered her breakfast.

She got up and closed the curtains, then had a shower and changed into pyjamas that smelled of home. To most people that would be comforting, but to her, home brought abuse to mind, nights spent crying, and planning murder. Once the police had left, she'd get cleaners in, new bedding and furnishings, and change the washing pods and softener to something else. Old smells had to go. She didn't want the memories going forward.

In bed, she stared at the space beside her where Henry would be and smiled at how empty it was. Light from the digital glowing numbers of the bedside clock she'd bought from home splashed fingers of light on what would have been his pillow, which was so smooth, and the lack of a head dent had her forcing down a burst of laughter.

It had happened. She'd got rid of him. Halle-fucking-lujah.

Spiteful memories came out to play, reminding her of what Henry had been like—she never wanted to forget, and recalling what he'd done to her would reinforce that she'd done the right thing. Yes, Riley had chosen him for her, she was happy to do what he wanted in exchange for money, but Henry had no right to treat her the way he had. He deserved to be dead.

While she was alone, she was free to feel exactly how she felt—happy he was no longer here—but when she went back out there, she'd have to pretend every second without him was agonisingly painful, that she would miss him forever.

But she sodding well wouldn't.

A message tone stabbed into the air from inside her bag. Who was that? She snatched up her bag and stared at the lit screen of the burner Riley had given to her.

YOUR PHONE WILL RING IN ONE MINUTE.

She gasped. The prearranged words. She placed a hand at the top of her chest, the coolness of her palm turning hot and sweaty with the flood of adrenaline. She hadn't expected that message yet, but she'd known it was coming. She'd thought it would have been in the next few months, not now. What had changed?

The phone rang, and she jumped a mile, although she couldn't stop grinning.

"Hello?" she said.

"Hello, my favourite woman."

"This…won't it complicate things, happening so soon?"

"I grabbed the opportunity while I could."

She smiled and imagined him also in the darkness, like they were when they stole moments together. "Okay, I suppose with Nathaniel dead now, it could look like the people who killed Henry went straight for him afterwards."

"Yes, and who cares anyway, you've got that lovely alibi of the hotel."

"I do. Why did it happen so quickly?"

"Nathaniel was involved in my Cara being killed."

"*What*? When did that happen? Why didn't you say sooner?"

"I'll tell you about it some other time. I need to ditch this phone and prepare to take over the Greaves Estate."

The line cut off.

Cara, dead? What the fucking hell had gone on? Had Nathaniel discovered Karen had been having an affair with Jonty/Riley so he'd taken away one of the things Jonty loved above all else?

She'd known Nathaniel had a nasty side to him, it had shown up on so many occasions during the planning of Henry's death, and it didn't surprise her one bit that he'd gone this far if he'd discovered one of his toys had been taken away from him.

But he was always destined to be killed by Jonty or his men.

She sighed. Her chat at the police station was going to look very different tomorrow — or maybe she'd receive a visit tonight. She supposed it depended on when the body was found.

Chapter Thirty-One

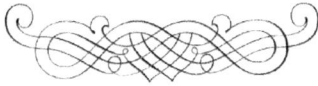

5:15 a.m. Colin was getting a bit pissed off now—or maybe it was that the case had grown another pair of legs which meant he'd be juggling extra balls and having to watch what he did and said more carefully. Another body had been found, and he didn't need a wallet with identification to know who it was. Nathaniel

Greaves, naked, gutted, and placed on grass, just like his father. No bakery with its tormenting scents nearby, though, which was something.

The chosen area consisted of an expanse of grass, a duck pond to the left, some wooden bench table sets to the right. A picnic area, where locals could pretend they were somewhere else for an hour or two, especially on a day like today. Trees cordoned it off from what lay beyond—a housing estate split into two parts, the poorer and the richer.

There were going to be a lot of narked people when they found out they wouldn't be allowed to sunbathe here today, maybe not even tomorrow either. Tape had already gone up, on the other side of the trees and here, along the road, creating a huge circle around the crime scene. More PCs were here compared to yesterday, on cordon duty. The officer who'd discovered Nathaniel had been driving around on his usual route, so no civilian witness to calm down and take a statement from. SOCO were on the way.

The twins hadn't told him about this murder until an hour before the call from the station had come in. Colin had been woken by the burner phone ringing then cutting off, and he'd read their message, bleary-eyed and half asleep, but the words had soon woken him up.

GG: One of life's little surprises has popped up. Nathaniel's been electrocuted.

CB: What?

They'd gone on to explain things. He'd have to keep the investigation on the same track as before: gangland leader killed in possible turf war. God, he'd only been the actual leader for a few short hours. Did that mean Karen now took over? Or would someone else swoop in, maybe another leader whose manor butted against the Greaves Estate.

Standing in his shoe covers on the road beside the grass while he waited for Nigel to turn up, having told him he recognised Nathaniel, Colin swiped the back of his gloved hand over his forehead—the sweating had started already. Not surprising when the morning was warm—overnight had been sticky—and he baked inside an extra layer because of the forensic suit. The air seemed thick without the breeze of yesterday morning, and the scent of dried-out grass was back. Many a front garden was yellow rather than green, although the communal areas like this were still abundant. The council probably watered it or something.

He turned to look at the row of parked vehicles—three belonged to response, plus there was his car. The SOCO van had just arrived. Sunlight glinted off all the windscreens and chrome wheels. He'd bet his bonnet was raging hot.

Forensic officers got ready in their outer clothing while Colin had a chat with Sheila Sutton, the crime scene manager. She hadn't been on duty yesterday.

"I'll get you caught up." He explained the familial link and how he suspected both men had been killed because of a grudge. He'd keep planting that seed wherever he went—the more people who had that in their heads, the more that line of thought would be the first one people brought up in conversations.

"So someone's taken umbrage with father and son, likely because they're leaders of an Estate—or maybe there's other family members to look at."

"No, the only one left is the wife, and she's distraught enough about Henry, so I dread to think what she'll be like today."

"Poor woman. Is this her son?"

"No, her stepson, but they're a similar same age."

Sheila raised her eyebrows.

"I know what you're thinking," Colin said, "but regardless of the father being old, she genuinely loved him. That's my take on her anyway."

"Rather you than me, breaking that news."

The scene sergeant turned up, and again Colin passed on what he knew, pointing him to the PC who'd found Nathaniel, and then lastly, Jim and Nigel pulled up at the same time. Nigel had bought breakfast again—maybe he'd had a personality transplant or something, or a secret pay rise. Colin chose a bacon roll and a cheese twist. They stood on the verge that ran alongside the cars, farthest from the crime scene, and ate their food with the bottom half still in the bakery bags so any debris didn't fall and create contamination.

"Was it the same as yesterday, he was gutted once he was brought here?" Nigel asked.

"Yes, and with no rain there's plenty of blood on the grass."

"Was he strangled?"

"No bruising around the neck that I could see, but he does have weird marks all over his body, something I haven't seen before."

"Do you think they're marks from being struck?"

"I'm not sure. They look sore, I know that much."

"Any broken fingers?"

"It doesn't look like he was tortured."

Jim waved now he was dressed up in his white overalls, and he walked over to where Nathaniel had been placed. SOCO worked around the body to put the tent up, a photographer snapping pictures regardless. Nigel and Colin continued to eat their breakfast. It was better to stay away for now; despite Jim waving them over, he could be grumpy if he had an audience when he did the initial checks.

"All the leaders except for one have been spoken to," Nigel said. "I stayed behind to do some overtime last night, I wanted news on alibis before I threw in the towel."

"Who wasn't available to talk? And is that a concern?" Colin already knew the answer.

"He's on holiday abroad, so unless that was one almighty planned alibi—and an obvious one at that—I'd say he had sod all to do with it. Doesn't stop him paying someone else to commit murder while he's soaking up the sun, though, and these gangsters have cash every-bloody-where, it seems, so there'd be no trail. But one of the other leaders said that the one on holiday was good friends with Henry, so he doubted very much it would be him. What were the twins like when you questioned them?"

"Too easy-going to have been up to something. There were two others who could corroborate their alibi, at least until two in the morning anyway, and they said they were together at home after that. We checked the route from The Angel, where they'd been chatting about renovating the pub, to their home, but sadly the one CCTV camera had gone kaput at around seven. That one fucks up a lot, apparently, according to a man called Bennett who works there. This was also backed up by another man call John."

"So you're happy it wasn't them."

"Yes."

"What about Jacob? What does he think? Not that I'm questioning your instincts or anything."

But you are, aren't you. "He found it odd that the twins didn't want to know why we were asking them for an alibi, but to be honest, if *I* hadn't done anything wrong, the last thing I'd be doing was asking questions which meant the police would hang around for longer. I'd want them gone."

"Same."

Sheila waved from over by the tent and gave them the thumbs-up—Jim was in a more receptive mood.

"Let's go then," Nigel said.

He took Colin's bakery bag and empty can of Pepsi Max, putting them in his passenger footwell. He blipped the car locks, and they walked over the grass. Someone had been stopped at the cordon, a jogger by the looks of it, who didn't appear too happy about being turned away, but that was tough shit.

Inside the tent, they each picked an evidence step to stand on to the right of Nathaniel and stared down at him. Jim, on the opposite side, crouched.

"Bleach again," Nigel observed pointlessly, sniffing. "God, it stinks."

"I think he's been electrocuted," Jim said. "If you look at the circular marks around the wrists and ankles, they look like burns instead of friction from rope. Then there's the marks on the rest of his body. It's very similar to someone I worked on who'd been struck by lightning. I doubt very much that's the case here, but I should imagine, when I look inside him, some of his organs may well be fried."

The idea of cooked gangster turned Colin's stomach.

"A different method of murder yet he was gutted and bleached just the same," Nigel commented. "Was the disembowelment to let us know the same people killed him?"

Colin didn't respond as it sounded like rhetorical musing. If he hadn't been working for the twins on this, he'd love to be able to say that different people tortured each man but the same person dumped the bodies then slit their stomachs, but he couldn't. It would not only be career suicide but he'd be nicked as a conspirator.

"Any note this time?" Nigel asked. "A wallet?"

Jim shook his head and stood. "No. He's still pretty soft in places, only just stiffening in others, so I'd say he was alive six hours ago, but don't quote me on it. I'll be sending the post-mortem report through for Henry this morning"—he gestured to Nataniel—"at some point when I get the chance to finalise it. Death by strangulation, as I suspected. Terrible business. He suffered a lot of pain with those fingers before he passed away."

Colin had found out last night at the Taj that Henry had been a pervert. When he'd learned that the man had abused his child in that way, probably only watching so he could pretend he wasn't a nonce because he hadn't touched, Colin had been glad the man was dead.

Nathaniel's death was a completely different kettle of fish—he was supposedly a kind and good leader, yet he'd ordered someone to murder two brothers, which had resulted in him also killing a leader's daughter. This news had come not so long ago on the phone from George. He hadn't said what had happened to Best, the killer, so Colin could only assume the man had been disposed of in the twins' usual way, or the other leader had got rid of him.

"Father and son, killed over two nights, their bodies both left in public places on grass," Nigel summarised. "Them being gutted, is it significant? Does it mean something? Or does the killer enjoy disembowelling people after torturing them for whatever reason? If the Greaves men were running their Estate in a nicer way than other leaders, then could that be the reason for their deaths? Did the other leaders feel Henry and his son needed to take a harsher road? Did their leniency mean that the residents thought they could do just what the hell they liked, on *all* Estates, and one leader in particular got pissed off with it?"

"It's certainly plausible," Colin said, "but we have the dilemma of them all having alibis."

"We'll look into the finances of the man on holiday, just as a paper exercise, but I really don't believe we're going to find anything that's going to point to a hitman being used. It's going to have to be door-to-door enquiries on the housing estate over there today, see if anyone saw anything happening during the night. I'll get the team in early at the station so they can go over CCTV."

"Any news back from door-to-door yesterday?" Sheila asked.

"Nothing, as it was only the parade of shops, and the people who live in the flats above were all asleep. I suspect the same is going to happen here. Killers who leave bodies out in the open don't do so if there's a risk of being seen—unless they want to be, of course."

Colin sighed. "I'll go and have a look if Jacob is around again today. I'll have to pay Karen another visit."

Nigel nodded. "You do that, cheers."

Chapter Thirty-Two

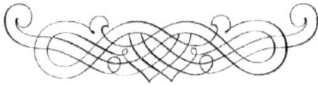

*D*ear Diary,

I've got to sneak out and meet Riley. Going by his angry text from a new phone, I think he's found out about Nathaniel. Fuck. I'm going to have to play this really carefully. Find out how he feels about me before I decide which of them I'll choose, which is the better option.

Who's the richest. And of the most benefit to me.

Love from,

Karen Marie Greaves

Henry was dead to the world after his sleeping tablets—three again—and she'd filled the evening with cleaning until it had got dark. The appointed meeting time was fifteen minutes away, so she left the street, cursing the loud exhaust of her convertible, something she'd loved when she'd first received the car as a wedding gift from Henry but not so much now when she needed to get away quietly.

She rolled up in the residential street opposite the park, getting out and blipping the locks, then rushing across the road, wincing as the gate screamed in protest. She went straight to the bench beneath the tree, waiting for Riley to come, the hour ridiculous, well past midnight.

He appeared in the distance opposite, striding across the grass as though his only purpose was to have a right go at her, and she couldn't blame him. It was one thing to agree to marry and fuck Henry, but his son, too? Was Riley jealous? Did he actually care for her like he'd said he did?

If so and they got married...think about all the money she'd have then.

She tried to draw in a long breath, but the humidity was so heavy she couldn't expand her lungs enough. There had been talk of storms coming, but none had materialised yet. Everywhere the grass was yellow, wildflowers wilting, their stalks bent as if they were exhausted. Despite it being the extreme early hours of the morning, she was so hot, sweat clinging to her skin, her silk blouse sticking to it.

Riley came to sit beside her, a silhouette in the darkness—he could be anyone, really. His smell gave him away, though, one of two aftershaves she'd become familiar with.

"What did you need to see me about?" she asked.

"Nathaniel."

"What about him?"

"He took me to one side earlier and said you were seeing each other. Is that right? And when were you going to tell me that you two had made plans of your own to kill Henry?"

"Why the hell did he take you to one side?" she asked. "Was there a leader meeting or something?"

"No, he was asking if I wanted to help him kill his father. I almost wet myself laughing, considering what me and you have been planning. I told him to ask the twins. They're batty enough to do anything."

"Right. What's it to you who I spread my legs for? You're probably playing me anyway, making out you care for me just so I'll stick to my side of the bargain. But let's face it, it's obvious I'm going to stick to it because I'm still married to the bastard and haven't killed him myself. I'm waiting for that fifty grand to drop at the end."

"And it will, I just need to know where I stand, because if you're thinking of running the Estate with Nathaniel… That was never the plan, Karen. You know exactly what I had in mind, taking it for myself, so why the hell are you fucking it up?"

"Has it ever occurred to you that I'm actually making things better by fucking my husband's son? This time next month I'm supposed to be dead, drowned in an Italian swimming pool then buried beneath grapevines. My husband's bored of me, wants me out of the way, so I had to take action without consulting you. And anyway, isn't it better that Nathaniel's the one to organise the murder, because if it all goes tits up then he's the one who'll get the *blame, then he'll be in prison and out of our way. Or should that be out of your way?"*

"You say that like you don't believe we're in this together until the end."

She didn't bother responding.

"When did you start shagging him?" he asked.

"I can't remember exactly when, but it's been a while. I've got him on side for our benefit."

"The thought of him touching you…"

"You didn't seem to mind when it was an old man doing it, and by the way, you're taking too long to get rid of the Carter brothers. You told me it'd be sorted, yet they're still alive. So Nathaniel said he'll deal with it. He's actually been setting everything up to make sure they disappear."

"You have to wait for the right time for these things, which is why I haven't done it yet."

"Yeah, well, a girl could think you're just using her, pretending you're going to kill her rapists just to keep her sweet, but I want them dead, Riley, and I'm going to get them dead, along with that Paddy fucking Winchester."

"What's he done?" He sounded shocked.

"He's been touching arses that he shouldn't be touching. I'm sick of perverts, my husband is the biggest one of them all with the way he treats me.

Paddy has to go. Me and Nathaniel have made plans, and I'm going to kill him—Paddy, not Nathaniel. I'm learning to be a leader's wife. Isn't that what you wanted, or was that more pillow talk?"

Silence rose between them, and she waited for what he had to say next when he'd digested the fact that Nathaniel was actually stepping up to the plate and Riley wasn't, although she wouldn't be telling Riley that the mission had been aborted regarding the Carters the other day. Nathaniel had explained—he'd made the right decision; there had been too many witnesses, and Best wouldn't have been able to get away quickly enough without somebody stopping him and possibly keeping hold of him until the police arrived.

"I haven't cared about someone for a long time," Riley said. *"Let alone allowed someone to keep calling me Riley when that isn't even my fucking name."* He laughed quietly. *"But I'm growing to love you—didn't expect it, just thought it would be a business transaction, but surely you knew my feelings were changing. Then when Nathaniel piped up about you earlier, I could've sliced his fucking face off. That's when I knew. I was jealous, and that means something. So if you're fucking around with him for our benefit, I don't want to hear about the times you've gone to bed*

with him, and if it's something more serious between you, then you won't see or hear from me again unless it's to do with our original agreement. So give it to me straight. What are you playing at?"

"I'm using him for us, for the future you told me you wanted."

He leaned across and kissed her. She kissed him back.

"I'd better go," he said and stood.

She nodded in the darkness. "Before you get questioned as to where you've been."

"Yeah, certain people have got a bit nosy lately."

Those people would be in her life, too, at some point. His kids.

He walked away, and she waited until he'd disappeared through a gap in some hedges before she got up and walked to her car. She got in and slapped the air-conditioning on, waiting for it to dry the sheen of sweat all over her. She gripped the steering wheel and squeezed it hard, telling herself she'd done the right thing in choosing Riley. Nathaniel wouldn't run the Greaves Estate in the way it needed to be run, so it was best he was dead along with his father so she could take over and Riley could run it for her behind the scenes, just like the original plan.

The way she had to keep waiting for things was starting to get on her nerves. She always had to calculate when this or that would happen, and every day she woke up, although it was closer to the endgame, it was still too far away. So what if she'd persuaded Nathaniel to help things along quicker. What did it matter when *Henry was killed, just that he was? Everyone had swallowed the fact that she loved him, she'd lied so convincingly, and when he snuffed it she could throw herself into the role of a weeping widow.*

She'd make it work.

She started the engine and drove away, towards the castle that would soon be hers and hers alone, something she'd probably sell if she were to move in with Riley. There was still so much to do before they reached that point, another couple of years before they revealed they were together, which was the lie she'd spun to Nathaniel about her and him, too—they played the mourning wife and son, then they just so happened to fall in love.

The stupid bastard had believed every word.

Chapter Thirty-Three

Karen sat on the Edwardian chair and stared out through the balcony doors. One of them was open, and a balmy breeze came through, warming her bare feet. She'd had a fry-up this morning but had asked for the trolley to be collected quite soon after she'd eaten—the smell of the food, she didn't want it lingering.

Colin sat on the matching chair in front of the window, and Jacob stood beside the dressing table with its fancy-framed mirror and complimentary cosmetics on a silver tray—a tiny tube of foundation, a thumb-pad-sized blusher compact, and a miniature lipstick. She'd known the other half lived like this because she'd been 'the other half' ever since she'd married Henry, but he'd never taken her to a hotel—they hadn't even had a honeymoon.

Colin had broken the news about Nathaniel in a gentle manner, and he looked across at her as though he worried she might crumble at some point and he hoped he wouldn't be there to witness it. Maybe he'd been through grief of his own, he certainly had that air about him, and he didn't want to watch someone else's for longer than necessary.

She wiped tears from her cheeks then used a tissue to dab at her eyes. "I've got a horrible hollow feeling in my chest." She laid a hand over it. "And my head throbs—probably from all the crying regarding Henry, and now this. I can't say I saw Nathaniel as my stepson because we're the same age or thereabouts, but I did see him as a friend, and he was so good to his father. We had a connection, maybe because of our ages and our mutual need to look after Henry, and I'm going to miss him. I don't think anything will ever make me whole again." She thought about the Atomic Kitten song and stuffed laughter down.

"I understand. Grief is an awful thing. When my wife died, I thought of it as an animal that had come to live inside me. An angry animal, then a broken one, and now it's very much a case of me living my life how she would have wanted me to. In time, maybe you'll be able to do the same."

She couldn't live how Nathaniel had wanted her to because that would mean he'd still be alive and running the Estate with her, and as for living as Henry had wanted her to, that would be on her knees, constantly attending to his cock. She shuddered.

"Are you okay?" Colin asked. "A stupid question, considering the news we've bought you this morning, but you shivered, so…"

"I was thinking of how awful it must have been for them both. I just don't understand it when they weren't the type to have enemies."

"The pathologist thinks Nathaniel was electrocuted."

"Oh my God!"

She'd known it was Jonty's method of murder, he'd described the process to her enough, explaining how the body fried eventually, and sometimes he kept going until the skin smoked. She imagined Nathaniel on the metal chair, wired up, ready to be cooked, and fought the smile threatening to emerge.

She forced her bottom lip to wobble. "I don't know what to say. It's all so...so...barbaric. It wasn't meant to happen like this."

"What do you mean?"

She realised then that she'd fucked up. Cold dread sluiced through her. For fuck's sake, she wished she wasn't dealing with this on her own. Jonty should have given her a warning about Nathaniel dying way before he had. She composed herself to steady her racing heart. "Well, they were both supposed to be alive, weren't they. My marriage wasn't supposed to end the way it did, and I most certainly didn't expect Nathaniel not to be here anymore. My *life* wasn't supposed to happen like this, do you understand what I'm saying?"

"Yes. We have all these plans, don't we, never expecting death to come calling and ruin it."

"Exactly that." *Thank God, I swerved a bullet.* "I'm not sure what to do now. Does that mean I'm left to run the Estate? I'll have to get hold of the other leaders, see what they have to say."

"There are women who run Estates. Jet Proust, for instance. Perhaps speak to her. She might be able to give you some pointers and help you along the way."

"Thank you, but I'm really not sure being a leader is for me," she lied. If the police thought she didn't want the job, then they wouldn't accuse her of arranging to have both men killed so she could take over.

"Would you like me to contact someone to sit with you, or would you prefer to be alone?"

"Alone, please. Although I'm not sure what to do now because Nathaniel booked this room, and I've been ordering room service, which he told me to because it would go straight onto his card. I don't know how long I'm here for, and I'd better contact reception to tell them to bill me for any food going forward, because surely it's illegal for me to knowingly put something on a dead person's account." She'd rambled on purpose. "Oh God, this is all so horrible. I have no idea when the police will be finished in the house either. It's like I'm completely lost and I don't know where to go for help or what to do and I...and I..."

"Take a breath." Colin smiled when she inhaled. "Forensics will likely be finished later today, and I'll check at reception for you to let you know regarding this room. If Nathaniel didn't prepay and he only left his card details on record, you could always go down and switch the bill to your card—assuming you've got one?"

"Yes, I have a bank card." She also had a credit card Henry hadn't known about, and she paid it every month from the allowance he sent to her via direct debit. Then there were the weekly grands she'd received, which she'd brought with her here inside a large vanity suitcase.

Colin stood, holding his hand out to shake hers. "Don't worry about getting up and seeing us out. I'll message you regarding my chat with the receptionist."

"Thank you. When will I be able to see Henry and Nathanial?"

"Someone will be in touch about that."

Colin moved to the door and opened it. Jacob gave her a nod, and then they were both gone, leaving her to bask in the warmth coming

EMMY ELLIS

through the balcony doorway. Five minutes later a message arrived. Nathaniel had paid for a two-week stay, so she decided she'd remain here, then Jonty could visit. She went down to reception to switch the card over for future room service, using the joint account debit card so it didn't come out of her own savings.

It wouldn't be long before everything in that account officially belonged to her anyway.

335

Chapter Thirty-Four

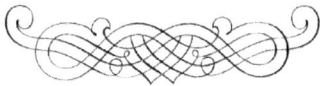

Colin had spoken to enough next of kin to know a liar when he saw one—the revelation (or the putting of her foot in her mouth) had come twenty-four hours late, that was all. Karen had been smooth when she'd covered up for what she'd said—"It wasn't meant to happen like this."—and what she'd said afterwards would put most people's suspicions to rest. But Colin wasn't most people. He hoped Jacob hadn't picked up on it.

Colin sent a message to The Brothers, telling them what she'd said and asking what she might have meant.

GG: MAYBE THAT NATHANIEL WASN'T MEANT TO DIE? BECAUSE HE WASN'T, AS FAR AS WE KNOW. HIS DEATH CAME ABOUT BECAUSE OF SOMETHING COMPLETELY DIFFERENT.

CB: I DON'T KNOW, IT JUST SEEMED MORE THAN THAT. MAYBE I'M READING BETWEEN THE LINES TOO MUCH. SHE SAID IT AFTER I MENTIONED THE ELECTROCUTION.

GG: NOW I SEE WHY IT SOUNDED SUSPICIOUS. LIKE NATHANIEL WAS MEANT TO DIE, JUST NOT IN THAT WAY.

CB: EXACTLY THAT.

GG: WE'LL ARRANGE FOR HER TO BE SPOKEN TO AT SOME POINT.

CB: GIVE IT A COUPLE OF WEEKS, THOUGH. LET THINGS DIE DOWN ON MY END FIRST. AND I DON'T WANT ANOTHER BODY ON MY HANDS.

GG: WASN'T PLANNING ON GIVING YOU ONE.

GG: Everyone keep your ears open regarding Karen Greaves. She made a little slipup with our copper today, quote—It wasn't meant to happen like this—said after she was told Nathaniel had been electrocuted. As far as we'd been told, she was in on this with Nathaniel, yet it sounds like he was also meant to die, just not 'like this'. Dodgy as fuck. What if she's engineered this somehow to get her hands on the Estate? We need to call a meeting in case she's planning to hand it over for someone else to run.

Jonty: I'm next in line, so whoever it is can do one. The Estate is mine.

Proust: Will keep an ear out.

Moon: [thumbs-up emoji]

More responses followed.

A worm of unease slithered in George's gut. What the *fuck* was Karen playing at?

Chapter Thirty-Five

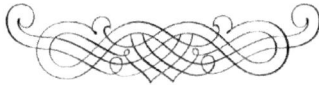

Two weeks had passed since Best had been dropped off at the hideaway flat. Despite killing Cara he was free, sort of, unless you counted him now being Jonty's latest bitch. After the man had calmly electrocuted Nathaniel, he'd turned to Best and asked for an explanation for how he'd come to know Nathaniel in the first place. The whole story had come out, how he'd been forced to work for him, the threats, everything. Jonty had decided that even though Best had pulled the trigger, he'd only done so under duress, knowing that if he didn't, Nathaniel might be the one to pull the trigger and Best would find a bullet square in the middle of his forehead, his brains decorating the wall.

Best had mentioned Tom, the factory, and the smelter that had been used to get rid of so many bodies he'd lost count, all the while Nathaniel pretending he was a good leader who didn't resort to violence.

Best had seen a completely different side to him than he'd shown others.

Jonty had arranged for one of his men to drop Best off at the flat so he could keep out of the way for a while, until he was needed for a job, one that would initiate him into Jonty's gang.

That job was in half an hour.

With his fake beard in place and dressed all in black, Best drove a stolen Transit to the other side of the Greaves Estate where a large house sat in its own grounds with a tropical back garden.

Chapter Thirty-Six

Karen sat on her new bed in the spare room, which she'd commandeered as hers. She'd had the one she'd shared with Henry gutted, planning to turn it into her office. She'd employed a man to come in and find all of the hidden cameras in the house. There had been eleven—even in the bathroom. She'd shuddered at the thought of Henry watching her in there, where things were supposed to be private. She'd left the CCTV cameras front and back outside, always checking the app if someone rang the bell or knocked.

There was a leader meeting due in two days, where she'd meet everyone and discuss her plans for her Estate going forward.

They were actually going to let her have it.

The familiar sound of the creaky floorboard in the hallway filtered upstairs, slicing through the quiet in such a way that it sent a cold sheet of ice through her body. Someone had put their weight on the floor and then stood still—she knew that because the second half of the groan hadn't happened yet. Then it came, low and long with the quiet tap of someone moving down the hallway.

Fingers of fear crept through her, the hairs on the back of her neck standing up, goosebumps spreading on her arms and legs and even her scalp. She hated feeling like this, especially because this time it wasn't a planned break-in. She tried to remember whether she'd locked the front door when she'd come in from town or if she'd just left it on the latch. Foxy had been here earlier, leaving behind his shears, so perhaps he'd come back for them. But this late?

She stood frozen to the spot, unable to move even if she wanted to, unsure what to do anyway. She switched on the app to see who'd entered using the front door. A man was on her screen, or she assumed it was a man because of the build, but she could only see him from the angle of the top of his head downwards. A balaclava covered his face and hair, his clothing dark, as were his thick-soled boots, the front of which were shiny from the light of the lamp next to the front door.

Her nerve endings tingled with fear, her mind a scrambled mess of not knowing whether she should get up and hide or run downstairs and try to go out the front way if he'd gone to the back of the house. She knew exactly which floorboard to dodge so he wouldn't hear her.

She listened carefully. More footsteps, except they were quieter, muffled.

He was coming up the stairs.

In the silence where he must have reached the landing and paused, the sound of her heart filled her ears, then the footsteps came again. Her brain screamed that someone had walked into her house as if they had every right, and they'd clearly checked the ground floor before coming up here. To find her?

She held her breath as the bedroom door slowly opened.

A gun came into view first, then the sound of its pop. She stared in shock at the dart sticking out of her chest, the pain of it entering her skin registering a second before she knew something wasn't right: sleep was coming, so quickly, and there was nothing she could do to stop it.

The last thing Karen had ever expected was to be sitting on the floor of a factory she'd been told about with a smelter that scoffed bodies so they were never seen again. She'd got a delicious thrill when Nathaniel had described it to her, but it wasn't so thrilling now that she faced it after being told she was going to get inside while she was still alive.

The man probably thought she didn't recognise him with the balaclava on, but she'd looked into his eyes enough times to know exactly who he was. Best. He'd locked the door that led out to the factory, so there was no escape.

He stood behind her, close enough for his hot breath to baste the back of her neck. She was about to move so the stream of air didn't hit her, but he came to stand in front of her. She stared at the man who had, for a while, been her ally. Now, he was no longer the helper she'd known but an executioner, she was certain of that. She glared at him, and his eyes flinched inside the holes of his mask. Didn't he like the way she tried to stare right into his soul and force him to admit he'd betrayed her, when she'd been willing to let him stay alive?

He moved to stand behind her. Probably didn't have the courage to look at her anymore.

Where was the life that was supposed to flash before her eyes? No flickering montage played out from her birth up until now. Instead, she had to bring things to mind herself. Dad getting ill. The kids at school bullying her. Dad dying—*the wrong fucking parent*! Her mother wallowing in grief and setting up a fatal alliance with Mr Vodka.

Karen searched for a tendril of remorse, a whisper of guilt, but…nothing. No regret for the choices she'd made. Each one had been justified at the time. There was no shame, buried deep, popping out now to torment her. No voice whispering that she was going to Hell—she'd known there was no place in Heaven for her. She had lived by her own rules; her life's ledgers were packed full of incidents, all of them written by her. She never had got around to burning them.

"I suppose this is where I beg you to spare my life," she said dryly. Really, she ought to be raging, so *angry* that it had come to this, but she couldn't find the energy to be arsey.

"I wouldn't be allowed to spare you," he said. "You know how this goes."

"I know. Why are you doing this to me?" she said, her mind still groggy from whatever had been in the dart. She remembered putting her signature on a couple of things, more than a couple, but for the life of her she couldn't remember what they were. She'd also accessed her banking apps—she recalled her phone screen being fuzzy.

"Jonty says goodbye," he answered.

Ah, so he betrayed me in the end, like I thought he would.

The shove to her back sent her flying forward. She instinctively put her hands up to brace her fall, but he pushed her again. The top of her body raced towards intense heat, then he lifted her ankles, and a suffocating hotness obliterated all thoughts.

Chapter Thirty-Seven

Jonty smiled when he got the news. Best would soon be dropping off the papers Karen had signed, which said she'd handed all property over to him.

According to the twins, who'd been keeping an ear out on their Estate and via their copper, already the Greaves' murders had been relegated to the back burner, and it wouldn't be long before they were forgotten completely, the deaths put down to some gangland beef or other.

Just the way Jonty liked things, all squared away like that.

He'd leave Karen's house empty for the time being, waiting for the heat to really die down, and Best would also be bringing her phone, so Jonty would answer any messages she received as though he was her.

All so it looked like she was still alive and had moved away.

While she'd been under the influence of the drug in the dart, she'd also transferred all money from a few bank accounts into one that wasn't in Jonty's name but it was his nonetheless; the money would go from there into another two accounts before the trail went cold, should anyone be looking.

Karen's life had ended right where it had started, in Skint as Arseholes Lane.

He'd played a fucking blinder.

He'd renamed the Greaves Estate as soon as the announcement had gone out that he'd taken over. It was now the same as his, Worth, and people were going to find that he was a very different leader to the two they'd not long lost. It was going to be a hard road without Cara in his life, but he still had Ben, and they'd be busy enforcing the rules.

One strike, and you're out.

He tucked away the part of him who had been Riley and smiled, ready to move on.

Chapter Thirty-Eight

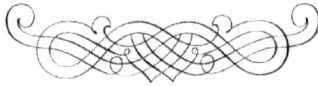

Tom Best sat on the riverbank with his wife, Louise. She held their baby daughter on her lap. Billie slept, her little cheeks flushed. They'd used factor fifty sun cream every half an hour, so maybe her face was red because she was so hot.

"I'll pop her in the buggy under the sunshade," Tom said.

Louise handed the baby over, and with Billie settled, still sleeping away, Tom put his arm around Louise. It was days like this he wished Shaun would come out with them, but he'd said this wasn't his cup of tea, sitting on the grass and getting sunburned.

To be honest, Tom hadn't really been a sun worshipper until Louise had taught him that it was okay to rest and enjoy a bit of nature. She said the vitamin D was good for him anyway. He had to admit that everything looked so much brighter and happier when the sun shone. Colours were more vibrant, and Louise's red hair had a beautiful sheen to it.

He traced the pattern of one of the squares on their tartan picnic blanket and thought about having a nap, but Louise wouldn't be too happy; she said they didn't see each other enough as it was.

A peal of laughter from a child running up and down the bank had Tom checking to see whether Billie had been woken up by it, but she slept on, content. A bee came over and landed on a daisy by his foot, and he had this great sense of peace come over him, that he was exactly where he needed to be.

On the water, a team of rowers went by, their synchronisation mesmerising to watch. The glistening water parted for their boat, ripples jostling towards the shore. They'd chosen a sandy area for today having driven to the South Bank, and it gave the impression they were at the beach. When Billie was older she'd be able to make sandcastles.

The scent of sweaty sandwiches, cheese Tom would bet, wafted towards him, and it reminded him they hadn't eaten their lunch yet, too intent on making sure Billie had her bottle first. He unpacked the baguettes he'd bought in the bakery this morning, passing one to Louise.

"Thanks," she said and smiled at him.

That smile always gave him butterflies.

A proper shrill scream broke the perfect tranquillity and had Tom on his feet in an instant. He dropped his lunch to the picnic blanket as he saw what others were looking at on the sand.

"Stay there," he told Louise.

He moved forward, reaching other bystanders who'd formed a wall so the children couldn't see. Tom elbowed his way in, and he stared down at a bloated arm, severed cleanly just below the elbow, and he recognised the ring on the middle finger.

Fuck.

To be continued in *Rioted*,
The Cardigan Estate 44

Printed in Dunstable, United Kingdom